To Carmine,

Going to See the Leaves

❧ ❧

with best wishes

Linda Collins

March, 1986

GOING

TO SEE THE

LEAVES

❧ ❧

Linda Collins

VIKING

VIKING
Viking Penguin Inc., 40 West 23rd Street,
New York, New York 10010, U.S.A.
Penguin Books Ltd, Harmondsworth,
Middlesex, England
Penguin Books Australia Ltd, Ringwood,
Victoria, Australia
Penguin Books Canada Limited, 2801 John Street,
Markham, Ontario, Canada L3R 1B4
Penguin Books (N.Z.) Ltd, 182–190 Wairau Road,
Auckland 10, New Zealand

First published in 1986 by Viking Penguin Inc.
Published simultaneously in Canada

"When the Pipes Froze" originally appeared in *Commentary*, "Fears"
(originally titled "A Nighttime Story") and "Going to See the
Leaves" in *The St. John's Review*, "Meditation on Play, Thoughts on
Death" in *The Hudson Review*, and "Intimacy"
in *Mademoiselle*. "Driving Back from the Funeral" originally
appeared in the *Kenyon Review*, V. VIII, No. 1.

The author is deeply grateful to the Corporation of Yaddo
for their support.

LIBRARY OF CONGRESS CATALOGING IN PUBLICATION DATA
Collins, Linda.
Going to see the leaves.
Contents: Changes—
When the pipes froze—Driving back from the funeral—
A family story—[etc.]   I. Title.
PS3553.047492G6   1986   813'.54   85-40624
ISBN 0-670-80881-4

Printed in the United States of America by
R.R. Donnelley & Sons Company, Harrisonburg, Virginia
Set in Linotron Bembo

FOR ARTIE

CONTENTS

The Doctor's House

◝◝ "Well, which one does? Enjoy it more? Do *you* say?"

"Woman," answered Sybil, turning to them all and laughing. "How mad you are. Not to know."

A woman of his own age, he had to say, nearly forty, having seen her earlier in the day, in the office under fluorescent light, and in the street in daylight on the way to lunch, but right now quite voluptuous, leaning back on the couch under the lamp in some kind of pinkish silk that rippled over her body and lent its flush to her face as she looked triumphantly from one to another of the guests, the male guests, that is; the women she seemed scarcely to see. Sybil McAllister, but part Maori, she had said, from Auckland, a solicitor, here with members of her firm for the closing of a piece of business, which closure was now being celebrated in his, Charles Hamilton's, thirtieth-floor apartment with its moleskin couch and greenish glass coffee table, its Pollock drawing and little de Kooning oil and the large uncurtained windows through which you could see, despite the thickly falling snow, the lights of the bridges and the buildings of the far reaches of the city.

"But how can you *know?*" asked the little wife of Philip Letwin, the accountant. She was sitting in one of the white molded chairs; her pregnancy jutted against the folds of a gray flannel jumper, her pocketbook lay across her lap. She frowned. "You can't know what someone else experiences. How can you?" She addressed the question to rosy Sybil on the couch but her tense voice went unanswered.

"Ah, indeed, how can one know the pleasures of fishes?"

intoned Rutherford, the partially retired senior partner, bowing gallantly in Mrs. Letwin's direction. Simon Rutherford's pleasures, reputed to have been at one time extensive, were now confined to his collections: of first editions, of porcelains, both Chinese and German, and of wine. He had once said to Charles Hamilton, in a taxi, that at the age of seventy he had exchanged his carnal interests for the pursuit of Orientalia. "I quite agree, Mrs. Letwin," he added.

Marcia Letwin cast a suspicious glance in the direction of the old man, of whose importance she was quite certain, having identified him from Phil's dinnertime descriptions, and wondered if she was being mocked. Had he implied that women were fish?

"A most philosophical remark of yours, my dear," he said. Rotating his wrist, he watched the remains of his drink circle about at the bottom of the glass.

Charles Hamilton, as the host, and also because he tended to be observant of tone and nuance, a tendency that had played a considerable part in his success as a lawyer, had noticed Marcia Letwin's mistrustful eyes enlarged by her curved thick lenses as she responded to Simon's affected gallantry, which barely masked, or so Charles thought, some hostility to the poor girl, springing either from the simple fact of her pregnancy or perhaps from her provenance alone. Simon was now adjusting his splendid cuffs.

Well, it was time for them all to go, thought Hamilton, deciding not to pour more cognac. The party was over, it had run its course. Now there was nothing to do but hope that Sybil could be kept from streaming out with the rest and might be persuaded to stay for a bit. There were signs that she might. The entire overseas contingent had checked out of the hotel. All its bags sat in his front hall—all, that is, but Sybil's, which were at this moment sitting on his bedroom carpet. He stood up and crossed to the far end of the room, where he bent and switched on the light of the fish tank. The light, filtering through water, waving water plants, mossy algae, and the translucent parts of the hanging fish, glowed softly.

"There you are, Simon," said Charles Hamilton. "The pleasures of fishes."

"Ah, glorious," sighed Sybil, with her arms extended and her head thrown back.

Everyone had turned to that bright object at the dark end of the room.

"It's my magic lantern," he said. And they did look like people in a theater, all eyes turned his way. Charles glanced at Sybil, who, while they looked away from her to see what that green light was, put her fingers to her lips and having kissed them gestured that she was offering the kiss to him. All right, thought Charles, she'll stay.

"Well, which?" asked Sybil, sitting up and leaning over him in the dim light.

"Well, which what?"

"Man or woman?"

"Man," breathed Charles through half-closed lips. Her face hung over him and her disarranged hair was orangy in the light of the little bed lamp. Dark curls with a glint snaked around her head. Her smiling lips were black. "What did you do to me?" he asked. She lay down beside him and rested her hand upon his thigh.

"Darling, I'm glad," she said. "You see," she said, "it's better to receive than to give."

"I'll bear that in mind," he said, closing his eyes. Would she go soon? he wondered. Would it turn out to be necessary for him to take her to the airport, or would she discreetly attend to herself in the bathroom and slip away, her bag dangling, calling good-byes in her stagy voice, cooing yet strident, like a mourning dove? He hardly dared hope so, but hope so he did. The fact that she had so taken charge in the sexual passage that had transpired between them seemed reason enough to think she would not need

5

to be escorted in a taxi all the way out through the snowy night to the departures terminal. She had enjoined him to passivity by suggesting that she be the barrister and he the clerk, a reversal he found hard to sustain, but each time he, impelled by use or need, attempted to initiate the next step, she had in one way or another urged him to give over the lead. And, one way or another, it had turned out well, very well indeed.

"But now I must go. Into the snow and the night, like the proverbial whatsit."

"I'll take you," said Charles, without moving.

"Out of the question. Not in the contract. But one thing. One last request."

"Anything," said Charles. "What?"

"I must see a photo of your wife. Your erstwhile wife."

"In the dresser drawer."

"The what?"

"The top drawer in the back," he said.

"Oh, the commode," said Sybil. "I don't see it."

Charles heard shuffling. He opened his eyes to the discomfort of the too-bright light to see the buttocks and soft arms of this woman foraging in his bureau drawer. "It's in a frame," he said.

"Ah *ha,* here it is." She switched off the overhead light and swiftly returned to the bed, where she crouched beside him, holding the picture close to the table lamp. Her breasts hung down. Charles was reminded of figures seen in the dimmer recesses of the Natural History Museum.

"I need me specs," she said, feeling for them without raising her eyes from the photograph of Amanda. She looked for a long time and he watched her, wondering what she would say.

"I don't see anything," she said at length. She put the picture down. "What was it? Did she slip off with the man in the motorcar?"

"She had to find herself, she said," said Charles, "and the search took her to law school and then to Washington,

6

where she now works for the Environmental Protection Agency."

"Ah," said Sybil. "I should have known. Well, sweetie, you must let me be off or me plane will be up and gone without me. Be a love and call a taxi."

She dressed in the half-light. He put his glasses on to watch her.

"Do you mind," she said, fastening her brassiere, with her back to him, "calling the airport, there's a sweetie, to see that the planes are flying in this weather? And then I'll just tiptoe away."

Dressed, she sat on the edge of the bed and kissed him.

"Good-bye," she said. "Happy Christmas. Don't get up."

When he heard the door to the outside hall close, he got up and stood naked at the window and watched the cab come to a stop. He observed the doorman's umbrella dip and in his mind's eye he saw the figure of Sybil bend to enter the cab. He heard, or imagined he heard, the car door slam. He watched the taxi glide to the corner, where the traffic light turned it a blurry red and then a watery green. When the cab was out of his sight, he stood back from the cold window. He saw the park was filling with snow.

He slept long and hard and his sleep was full of dreams. He dreamed all night long, and in the morning, as he woke, he had the distinct sense of rising through fathoms of space until he came to himself in bed.

Later in the morning, at the office, he heard that the large group of travelers was fine and awaiting a connecting flight in San Francisco, but Sybil, he learned, had perished in a crash at O'Hare Airport, to which her flight had been rerouted, the plane having evidently, at least according to early reports, flown into turbulence, lightning, and winds of extraordinary velocity. He was shocked, of course, but not grieved. To be perfectly factual, he hadn't known her at all, but he shuddered to think that only hours before she had fallen to earth and died in flames, he had looked

up at her coppery face and the hair that had switched from
black to red and had brushed against his chest as she moved.

In January, Charles had planned to take a short vacation,
to Barbados, with his old friend Douglas Crawford, who
happened to be his internist, as well. The evening before
they were to leave, however, Charles was informed by
telephone of Simon Rutherford's sudden death. Rutherford
had collapsed in the loft of a young woman whom, it
seemed, he was visiting in order to examine terra-cottas
of some interest but of dubious, even shady, origin. "That
throws *your* theory into a cocked hat," murmured the young
voice of Peter Woods, Simon's assistant and the bearer of
the news. Charles reflected that he was very junior indeed
to be speaking thus. The trip had to be canceled, of course.
That is, Doug went alone, while to Charles fell the task
of speaking to the *Times* and to the police and of calming,
by the tone of his voice and the deliberate pace with which
he moved about the office, the shock that was evident
everywhere in the firm. Charles felt quite stern when he
observed the attentiveness with which the clerical staff
looked at him, as though he might tell them something
interesting about it all. To set an example of decorum, he
declared he would at once write a letter of sympathy. He
was standing at the window looking out while he felt for
the right tone when he asked himself to which of Simon's
wives should he write. Or should he write to them all?
But so doing would increase rather than decrease the suggestion of morbid ribaldry the news of Simon's death had
provoked. He decided to write only to the children, and
thereupon called in Karen and dictated to her five (having
ascertained it was in fact five) letters, each slightly different
from the last. When she brought them to him, he reflected
he ought really to have written in longhand, but then he
thought, To hell with it, and gave them back to her, signed.
     At the funeral, Charles sat with the members of the firm,

just behind the family. Only one of the wives came, the first, she was believed to be, quite an old lady, and of the children Charles was not quite sure: two came, at most three. Charles sat in the pew and continued to feel stern.

In February, Marcia Letwin was delivered of her child. Letwin was suitably joyful. It was a son, and it was christened (so to speak, thought Charles) John. Letwin had participated in the birth in various ways. He was virtually quivering with happy excitement. Charles was much relieved when Letwin went back to his desk. At the end of the day he asked Karen to go to Tiffany's and order an engraved silver cup. In due time he received a letter from the new mother, thanking him for the present and inviting him to come and see the baby. Charles noticed that she spelled the child's name *Jon* and realized that on the cup it had been misspelt.

In March—the twenty-first of March, the date was written in his blue appointment book, a dark day in which the sky never cleared at all—Charles went to see Doug Crawford about his abdominal distress, dizziness, and other troubling systems, for the second time. The fact that his discomforts had not cleared up of themselves but had, if anything, intensified since his previous visit made him fearful that something grave was the matter and caused him to attend closely to his physician's expression while he was examining him. This time Doug took it all rather more seriously. He drew a good deal of blood, asked for what he called a midstream sample, and instructed Charles in its production. Discreetly, knowing his patient's sensitivity, he stepped away from the examining room with its adjacent toilet and walked down the corridor to the waiting room, where he leaned over Claire's shoulder and pretended to look over the open pages of *A Week At A Glance.*

9

He then returned to his office and told Charles to get dressed.

"I want you to have a chest X-ray," he said, "and see Ahmed Haroun for a sonogram."

"Haroun?" said Charles.

"First-rate," Doug said. "Absolutely first-rate. It's a new procedure. Fairly new, that is. And it will obviate the need for a lot of nastier procedures. It's just a sonic sort of thing. A sounding."

"Don't they do it for..." Hamilton hesitated, some vague association having been struck, something he had heard which he connected with someone at the office, the librarian, perhaps, but a former one, certainly not the elderly Miss Harris, who, he was confident, as was the entire firm, would not leave for reasons either romantic or maternal, and upon whom he, for one, had become quite dependent.

"For all sorts of things," Doug said briskly, not wanting to encourage him to linger on whatever illness his fears were settling upon. "Routine, at this point. Go straight there. I'll call him and tell him you're on your way. And when he's finished with you, you can stop off and have the X-ray."

He tore off two slips from his prescription pad, upon which he had written the addresses of the radiologist and Dr. Haroun, and handed them across the desk to his anxious patient. Standing up, he walked with him to the door and put an arm around his shoulders.

"But the nausea's gone, you say?"

"Completely gone."

"Well, we'll get to the bottom of this," said the doctor.

They shook hands and parted, the doctor to stand at his office window looking out onto Park Avenue, at the rain, the wet traffic, and the water flooding the gutters, until he saw his friend appear and walk to the corner, where he stood waiting for the light to turn with his head bent and the point of his umbrella placed in a crack in the sidewalk. While he waited, he moved the umbrella handle forward and back and then from left to right. He was clearly deep in thought. Worried, no doubt, thought the doctor, who himself believed under the circumstances that there might well be cause for concern. Well, he thought, let's hope not, and he buzzed Claire to send in the next patient, while he in the meantime called Haroun.

Dr. Haroun's office was between the Jewish Museum and Mount Sinai, an observation whose amusing implications Charles Hamilton might have developed under ordinary circumstances as he walked along, but today his anxiety preempted his thoughts. He reviewed the evidence: his various symptoms, none of which was dramatic or painful, had, it seemed, this time impressed Doug. Otherwise why the hearty tone, why the reference to "other procedures" and the dark hints of nastiness down hospital corridors? Why this expedition to the upper reaches of Fifth Avenue? Clearly there was reason for apprehension. He was unaccustomed to ill health; he was used to feeling well. At thirty-nine he was thinner than he had been ten years earlier: somewhat less flexible, perhaps, but with more stamina and better wind, the result, no doubt, of regular exercise, fewer martinis, and no cigarettes. And apart from the quite normal agitation he had suffered at the time of his divorce—he had had difficulty drawing a breath—he enjoyed an uneventful spiritual life as well. What was the matter with him? Was he caught already in that tangle of malfunction that waited to drag him through illness and pain to the end of his life? Fear swelled in his chest and flooded his body, through his arms to his hands, through his belly and down his legs. He stopped walking. He wished he didn't have to carry himself, crossing streets, stopping for lights, umbrella in one raised hand, briefcase in the other, through this series of appointments, but instead could sit down, or lie down. But he could not. Going home was out of the question. And the dizziness, the trouble, what-

11

ever it was, would follow him; he had given it time enough
to go away by itself if it was going to; two months, almost
three. But maybe not, maybe he hadn't given it enough
time, despite what Doug seemed to think. Standing still
under an awning, he rested the ferrule of his umbrella
beside his shoe. The doorman opened the heavy door of
the warmly lit lobby and looked at him with a decorously
questioning expression. Charles raised his umbrella and
started walking. The wind had subsided and the rain was
no longer being driven in slanting lines but was falling
gently. Under his umbrella it was quieter, and the umbrella
was easier to hold now that he didn't have to keep it upright
against the pushing wind. As he walked, he checked the
house numbers, and when he'd found the right building
he looked for the office entrance, just after the awning and
down two steps. Beside the door, a well-polished plaque,
oval, slightly convex and somewhat larger than a physician's ordinary doorplate, read A. HAROUN, MDPC. "All
right, Ahmed," said Hamilton to himself.

He told his name to the receptionist, who said, "Would
you spell that, please?" Not finding his name on her reg-
ister, she was preparing to send him away, when another
woman appeared and said, "Angela, it's all right. Dr. Haroun is expecting him." Angela looked up at her colleague
with a lift of her eyebrows. Her expression bespoke her
thought: Well, if we won't keep to our appointment list,
what is the point of going to the trouble of making it? But
the second woman, in her twenties, slender, wearing a pink
suit, leaned over Angela's shoulder and poked along the
rectangles of the appointment book with the eraser of her
pencil. The desk lamp lit their hair: the newcomer's fair,
Angela's black. They were like two women in a play, and
Hamilton watched them as though he was watching a
play. Angela was nineteen, Italian, perhaps, just out of high
school. Her lips were made up with glossy lipstick, and a
circle of rouge that did not hesitate to announce itself as

12

artifice stained her pale cheek. Her eyelids, cast down for the perusal of the appointment book, were violet. She was exceptionally pretty. Watching them as they studied the book, Charles felt he was waiting for something pleasant.

The older woman straightened. "Mr. Hamilton?" she said. "Dr. Crawford has just spoken to Dr. Haroun. If you will just have a seat, we will call you."

"I'll just slip him in here," she said to Angela and wrote with her pencil what Hamilton took to be his name.

His umbrella had left a pool of water at his feet, and his soaked raincoat clung to his shoulders. He deposited the one and hung up the other and turned to the magazine rack, from which he drew an assortment. Sitting down with the magazines in his hands, he looked around the waiting room and caught the glance of a heavily pregnant woman in galoshes, who at once returned to her book. Dr. Spock, no doubt, he thought. He prepared to wait. This is unendurable, he said to himself, after a few minutes, and started on the little speech he tended to polish in waiting rooms, the essay about courtesy, and time, and the assumption that the physician's time, or the dentist's, was of an order different from the patient's. His calm was leaving him but he held onto it as though to a fold of its skirt. He looked toward the receptionist's desk, where the telephone was ringing. Angela was not to be seen. Suddenly his magazines slid from his lap to the floor and he bent to retrieve them. As he raised his head a black frame appeared at the borders of his field of vision and threatened to invade the whole. Cold seized him. I am about to faint, he thought. Next he observed the strands of the beige carpet at too close a distance. I have fainted, he thought. He was lying with his nose in the carpet.

Their little cries and the rustle of their clothing told him that the two women had come to his rescue. The one in the pink suit wore a delicious perfume. When he was seated again Angela offered to bring him a glass of water and promised it would not be long now. He took a sip of water and put the glass down. He wondered just how long a wait it was going to be.

Called at last by Angela ("Doctor will see you now," she said, just as he imagined she would), he followed a waiting nurse with a clipboard down the corridor, passing a number of doors, some of which stood ajar. Averting his eyes from what might be within those doors, he could not help but look into the dark room at the end of the corridor in which he could see, despite the darkness, the gleam of the hall light shining on the edges of dials, wheels, and levers of the various pieces of apparatus inside, as well as the end of the bed, or rather the table, upon which he was going to lie. "Take off everything," said the nurse, who had stopped in front of an open door and was indicating with her free hand that he should go in. "Put the gown on with the opening at the back and open the door when you are ready." Inside the cubicle, he slowly took off his jacket, which was dark blue with a fine, almost imperceptible, stripe, and hung it on the hanger. He did the same with his trousers. This was, he reflected, the second time thus far he had undressed today. He watched himself in the mirror as he untied his tie, also dark blue, with little red dots, and then arranged the tie over the shoulders of his jacket. His shirt was still fresh and unwrinkled except around the waist where it had been tucked into his trousers. Standing in his underwear and shoes and socks, he backed away in order to see as much of himself as possible in the short mirror, but he could see only his face and part of his chest. He stepped closer and peered into the mirror. For a second he caught a glimpse of himself as a boy with wide round eyes and smooth cheeks and an expression that was soft and questioning. Instantly this look called to mind his mother, who had died when he was seven and who had, at least in the photographs he had of her, a similar expression, a tender and troubled look, as though, or so it had seemed to him as a boy, before he had decided not to think

14

about her, she knew she was going to have to die. He stood facing the mirror but no longer looking in until a sound from the hall reminded him of where he was and that his next task was the removal of the rest of his clothes.

At last, having put on the rumpled cotton gown with the ties in back and slid his feet into the paper slippers, he opened the door to the corridor and stood patiently waiting, feeling vulnerable because he was, in essence, undressed and yet at the same time content to place himself trustfully in the hands of whoever presented herself to take charge of him. It was the nurse with the clipboard who appeared and whom he followed to the door at the end of the hall, where he became, upon entering, the province of still another woman.

"Go up, please, Mr. Hamilton," said the new nurse. Obediently he climbed onto the table and lay down. Good office procedure, he thought, that she used his name. Good psychology. The room was quite dark and there were more people in it than he had first seen. In addition to the nurse, who was now arranging his limbs, a woman with her back to him was standing at a filing cabinet, and there was a man at the controls of the larger of the machines. The nurse at his side was small and had light, cold hands; she had curved lips and large nostrils, a delicate nose, and large round dark eyes. Filipino, he thought, and tried to think of something to say to her that would be provocative and yet not disrespectful and that, although coming from him lying on his back, would in one breath assert that he was a man and she was a woman, and that under other circumstances he might well be touching her limbs with a gentle experimental touch rather than she his. He would have liked in addition to find a way to tell her that his recognition of her as a person from the Philippines, if it was in fact the Philippines she came from and not somewhere else, Indonesia, for instance, carried with it no tinge of prejudice; everyone was aware that many of her people were working as X-ray technicians, as trained and re-

15

sponsible assistants to doctors. He was sure she was right to be proud of her job, and in no way did he mean to make light of the dignity and importance of her achievement by indicating that despite the asexual nature of their present confrontation, she was nonetheless to him a woman and he to her, he hoped, a man.

But he could think of no suitable way to say this, and in the meantime, she, after having made satisfactory adjustments of the position of the limbs on the left side of his body, came around to attend to the other side and discovered that he was holding in his right hand his wallet, his tie clip, and his lapis cuff links. "Oh, dear me," she said, holding her two small hands under his. "You must let them go. You must not worry about them. They will be right here." He let them fall into her hands and turned his head to one side to watch her put them on top of a metal cabinet where they were in view. "Women have their pocketbooks," she said, "but the men have nothing." She arranged his right side to her satisfaction and then drew the gown down over his body and smoothed it with little patting motions. "You must relax yourself now," she said. "Dr. Haroun will be here soon."

He wished she would not leave. He wished she would stay and chat with him while he waited for Haroun, but she stepped away and moved quickly across the room. She was wearing white trousers. She closed the door behind her.

Hamilton, who had been quite unaware that he was clutching his belongings in his hand, now that he was relieved of them, felt an ache in his wrist. He stretched his fingers and turned his hand this way and that. Bizarre, it seemed, that he should be forlorn at the departure of Miss Marcos, or whatever her name was, just a little creature doing her job. He was chilly. He turned his head to see whether the other people were still in the room and whether someone could be persuaded, for Christ's sake, to get him a blanket. "Excuse me," he said, but to no response. "Excuse me," he said again. There was indeed still someone bending over a desk at the far end of the room.

"Just a moment," answered a woman's voice. "Dr. Haroun will be here shortly." But her tone was brisk and Hamilton felt disenfranchised to place requests. He prepared himself to wait and closed his eyes, but the wait was short, for in a minute a voice behind him said, "Hah. I am Dr. Haroun," and he saw by casting his eyes above his head a face with glittering eyeglasses and shining teeth. The doctor circled around him and came to a halt. Two further faces appeared and with a low rumble of rubber wheels the many-wired apparatus was drawn up beside the bed.

"Now, my dear fellow," said Dr. Haroun, "we are going to listen to you presently and we shall see what we shall hear. But first you must be anointed."

Hamilton thought surely he had misunderstood, but evidently not, for all of a sudden hands were reaching over his abdomen and smoothing upon his exposed body something cold and oily. The substance, the grease, whatever it was, was stiffer than oil and stickier than Vaseline. It was cool at first but quickly felt warm. The hands slid over his chest and belly, moving from one side to the other and back in small even circles, missing none of him. He gasped.

"Breathe, sir," said a voice he recognized as belonging to the Filipino nurse. "Breathe, don't hold your breath." But it was almost impossible to breathe deeply and regularly as they wanted him to while his torso was being slid upon by two or possibly three pairs of hands. Dr. Haroun was standing at his feet and smiling pleasantly, with his arms folded across his chest, while he waited for the accomplishment of these preliminaries. "Yes," said Haroun, "it is much the best if you relax." However, as Charles felt fingers sliding into creases where he was accustomed only to the touches of amorous hands, a sensation antithetical, under the circumstances, to any chance

17

of relaxation seized him, and he mightily feared he might respond to it, but although there was such a danger, or so he thought for a minute, it was supplanted by another response. All at once the hands began to tickle, and his laughter spurted out. He tried, by closing his lips over his teeth, to suppress the laughter, but in vain. He snorted and sputtered. Although he tried to remind himself that these were medical people and all forms of incontinence were commonplace to them, he was quite unable to modify his embarrassment. He felt like a baby, like a frog, like mere protoplasm. It was all exceptionally unpleasant.

"Good," said Dr. Haroun. He was speaking to the nurses, who withdrew their hands at once. A second doctor appeared and stood beside Haroun. The dim lights went out, and except for the small red lights on the machine, the room was in darkness. Haroun leaned forward, holding in his hand an object that he commenced to pass over Charles's body, while talking rapidly to his colleague. Laughter had left Charles feeling tired and horrid. He closed his eyes.

It would have been more like Hamilton to be attentive, to watch, to ask intelligent questions. He knew the tone to take; it was second nature to him. It was a matter of establishing credentials and expressing interest without infringing on the physician's domain. You could, he knew, create an understanding that you were the sort who wanted to know the procedure, that you had some rudimentary sense of the mechanics of things, that basic science was not beyond your grasp, and that you and he were together in this, both of you educated people. It was not different with any professional. In his own office he was often struck by the fact that some clients simply put themselves in his hands, took no interest in the mechanics of their case, not just women, although for the most part it would take a woman to be so passive, but there was the odd man as well who, once the preliminaries were over, would sit back, so to speak, to await the outcome, keeping his anxious gaze on you but never once inquiring into the general principles, much less the finer points of the relevant statute. For Hamilton there was a pleasure in being on top of things. It extended to sports, to politics, to business. You read *The Economist, Scientific American, Sports Illustrated.* You knew how to navigate the skein of *peripheriques* between the airport and downtown Lyon, or Kansas City. You knew what camera to buy and whether to buy it in San Juan or Amsterdam. Hamilton didn't fool himself, as he thought some men did, that this expertise constituted anything profound. To hear the satisfying sound of your well-made shoes on the floor of the office corridor or the solid clunk as the car door slammed were not deep pleasures—to think so would be crass—but they did offer a kind of bitter comfort.

What would Charles Hamilton, greasy, lying with his eyes closed in a trough of calm between crests of mortal fear, have said was a sweeter comfort? He wouldn't have said. No fool, he knew that life has its beginning and its end. He knew there are no exemptions, no immunity, no privilege. What would he grieve to leave, if this were to be his mortal illness? His pale German automobile with the bucket seats? His Barcelona chairs? His Rothko? The suggestion would have made him snort. You do what you can, he would have said, and make the best of things. In a sense, life did not bear too much thinking about. He would never have believed when he was first married to Amanda, when he used to like simply to lie beside her and hold up strands of her hair to the light, that it would all come to nothing, that he would find himself taking women to restaurants, adjusting his tie in the elevator, feeling for his keys, all that. What might he have expected? Something less dry, with more of a gleam to it. Now he thought of himself as one among many, among the many who go about their business and do little harm, and that in itself was something, was it not?

"Ho!" said Haroun. "Ho?"

Charles heard a definite increase in the medical murmuring around him, but he did not open his eyes. What that murmuring augured, even when it was accompanied by rumblings and clinks as some additional machine was brought near, left him unresponsive. It would come out as it would. The sounds of quick footsteps and the rattling of metal reached his ears. Then there was silence.

"Mr. Hamilton?" It was the voice of his little brown-skinned friend. He opened his eyes. The room, except for the two of them, was empty, and the lights were on. "Doctor is finished. You may get dressed now," she said. Her eyes were huge in her tiny face, and she touched him on the shoulder with an icy hand. "I will clean you," she said and began to scrape the oily substance from his body, keeping, or so he thought, her eyes averted from his face. When she had scraped him to her satisfaction, she scrubbed his chest with a damp cloth. Suddenly she emitted a squeaky giggle. "Excuse me," she said. "Let me help you sit up, sir. You may be a little bit dizzy." Cradling his head, she pushed with her little body until he was sitting on the edge of the table looking down at his white feet. He was more than a little bit dizzy.

When he was dressed he picked up his briefcase and checked the cubicle to make sure he hadn't left anything. In the waiting room he drew his umbrella up through the cylinder of the brass umbrella stand and took down his raincoat from the coat rack. He laid the raincoat over his arm and smoothed its folds with his right hand. It seemed a long time since he had come into Dr. Haroun's waiting room from the street. He thought for a moment of sitting down and looking at a magazine for a bit before leaving. There seemed no reason not to. Two women looked at him and then returned to their conversation. There was a smell of wet wool. Whatever was wrong with him, he felt no fear. He had walked into this waiting room with the sentence of death laid upon him, but his fear had spilled off, and whatever Doug would tell him, good or bad, when the reports were in had no power over him. He was quite calm. He felt in his pocket for the paper from Doug's prescription pad with the address of the radiologist. The receptionist's desk was empty. Angela was not to be seen, nor the other one in her rustling clothing. He looked back one more time. Well, he thought, enough of this. On to Dr. . . . Dr. What? He peered at the paper but he would have had to fish out his other glasses to make out the name. He knew the building, he was set to go. He shoved the paper down into his pants pocket and went out into the street.

The radiologist's office was off Madison, several blocks down. It was still raining. The streets, the sidewalks, and the walls of the buildings had taken on a dark slick surface and a dark gleam. The sky was dark and the rain fell steadily.

In the lobby he took out the paper again and with his reading glasses read the name of the radiologist. He refolded the paper and rang where it said RING THEN ENTER. Then he entered.

To this receptionist he said, "I am Mr. Hamilton. I believe Dr. Crawford has called about me," but the receptionist, instead of suggesting that he sit down in the waiting room, said that he was to go straight back to Dr. Crawford's office.

"No chest X-ray?" he said.

"No," she said, importantly. Upon her desk was a pile of large manila envelopes, on the topmost of which was written in a felt pen *Mrs. Elena Garcia—Flat Plate of the Abdomen*. The receptionist put her hand on the pile as though to illustrate that he was being barred from the procedure. Behind her extended a long corridor. Along the walls Hamilton saw shelves, files, and the corners of envelopes similar to the ones in front of him. At the far end of the hall a young woman in white trousers and a white jacket was conferring with a colleague in a smock.

21

"Dr. Crawford called and said to cancel the X-ray and to tell you when you arrived to come back to his office right away."

Hamilton rejected the notion of telephoning Crawford, of using the girl's phone and straightening this out at once. Unlike Doug to unschedule X-rays, unlike him to betray panic, and Hamilton, discerning what he took to be panic in his physician's action, was himself once more very much afraid.

Claire, Doug's receptionist, said, "Go right in to him, Mr. Hamilton. He's waiting for you."

Doug did not appear, as he usually did, in the doorway of his consulting room, but as Charles entered he saw him standing instead at the window, bent slightly, with both hands resting on the sill, looking down at the street.

"Doug."

The doctor turned.

They sat. Charles waited. He thought of trying to say something that would make this easier for Crawford, whose face, to Hamilton's quick glance, looked strained.

"I do not know quite how to put this," said Dr. Crawford, in his quandary twisting his face so that his mouth appeared to have transferred itself from the midline to far into the left side, which had taken on a series of cracks and fissures while the right remained smooth. The grimace betrayed a mighty effort. At the sight, Hamilton wished to forestall the sobs, or whatever outburst threatened the tormented physician, and was trying his best to say something that would convey his capacity to absorb the force of whatever blow the man was obliged to deal, even if he were to announce his immediate end, so disturbed was he to see Crawford's manner fail in a medical crisis. It is the worst, then, thought Charles.

"It's OK, Doug," he said to his friend.

Dr. Crawford let out a short barking noise followed by

some choked sounds which developed into laughs. The man was laughing. Charles watched, trying to understand what death was foretold him in that laughter. There was nothing to do but wait. Presently the doctor regained control of himself. He reached for a tissue from the box on his desk, kept, no doubt, thought Charles, for patients in distress, and, extracting a fistful, patted his eyes and cheeks and wiped his mouth. Then he reached for more tissues to blow his nose.

"OK, fella. This is the poop," he said. "Haroun says you are in your second trimester. He says you are almost four months pregnant."

Hamilton looked at Crawford. What was this? What Doug said made no sense. But Hamilton, as he heard the words, had the impression of something rushing toward him. The meaning of the words, that something strange and profound had already begun to happen to him, presented itself in the form of a small round object, no larger than a man's hand, which burst into existence at a point in the room near the window and was swiftly moving through the air to where he was sitting. As one sometimes recognizes people or things without ever having seen them before, so Hamilton lost no time in disbelief. The idea of a pregnancy, an idea which naturally he had not previously entertained, became a fact at the moment his old friend pronounced the words. This is strange, he thought, but it is true. Why did I not think of it before? He felt his past life shrivel. Fear of what lay before him caused him to sit still and bend his head. He didn't notice that Crawford was still struggling to smooth his badly deranged composure.

Charles raised his head and looked trustfully at his friend.

Crawford shuddered. On his desk was Hamilton's folder: quite a full file it was, going back ten years at least. He was trying to render the various sheets of paper and unevenly folded laboratory reports into a neat pile by holding the stack loosely in his hands and tapping first the long

23

side and then the short against his desk blotter. He was trying to do this without looking, and some of the sheets slipped out from the pack and made him have to start again.

"Haroun is quite sure," he said. "For an Arab, that is," he muttered. "Bastard," he said.

"Bastard?" asked Hamilton. "Why bastard?"

"Figure of speech," said Crawford. "He is quite sure. He had them do a hurry-up. . . . But let's have a look at you." He started to rise as though to lead the way to the examining room, but his expression changed and he sat down again. "Actually, no," he said. "I think I'll let Millspaugh take a look at you." He paused, fingering his prescription pad. "No," he said after a minute, without looking at his friend, "not Millspaugh; Feldman," Feldman being the obstetrician to whom he made referrals in cases where there was any question of difficulty; otherwise he sent everyone to Millspaugh right here in the office. He would send Charles to Feldman. And not have anything more to do with this . . . charade, was what he was thinking, as he swiveled back and forth in his desk chair. He turned his eyes to meet Hamilton's and saw in them the deep gaze of someone whose attention is fixed on an inner horizon. Hamilton turned away and leaned against the arm of his chair. His raincoat, heavy with damp, hung in deep folds from his lap. His head was bent toward one shoulder and the shoulder was raised a bit toward his cheek, as though he would shrink in upon himself. Beneath his knit brows, his sideways look was sober, even severe. Crawford, observing a softening of the angle of his jaw, saw that a change had indeed taken place. He stood up abruptly, then bent over the desk to write Feldman's name and number. He looked at his watch. He calculated that if he were to pass lunch and shave it close at the hospital, he could get in a short game of squash. He felt he could well use it. At the same time, it seemed exceptionally difficult to hustle his old friend out onto the street, much as he would have liked to do just that, hustle him out and set him on some completely other chain of medical referrals so that the whole issue would be out of sight and thus out of mind, out of mind, that is, until it showed up in the *New England Journal*. Or, what was more likely, in the *National Enquirer*. Briefly, he considered writing the freakish thing up for the *Journal* himself. In a way, he thought, it would be quite something. He looked speculatively at Charles. No, he thought. Impossible. A friend, after all.

"All right. Let's go eat something," he said, calling upon his sense of decency to help restrain himself from adverting to some unforeseen hospital duty and hurrying off.

After the last time Hamilton had come into the office, they had had lunch at their university club, but this time Crawford, unaware that he was doing so, steered them, once they were on the street, toward Lexington Avenue. Hamilton, however, resisting the pressure of Crawford's hand on his arm, turned back toward Park Avenue and began to look around for a taxi. Crawford understood that Hamilton had in mind to repeat their previous lunch, whereas he, he realized, was urging his friend toward a quick bite in some dark place where they could eat without being seen. He increased the pressure on Hamilton's elbow. Charles turned obediently around, and they tucked their heads down and pushed into the driving rain.

Seated in a booth, they dried their eyeglasses.

"Liver and onions?" asked Crawford, when their martinis arrived. "How does that grab you?"

Hamilton looked at him as though he had not understood. A gust of damp had come in with them. In the restaurant, the air smelled of vegetables cooked a while ago: string beans, cabbage, boiled onions, Brussels sprouts, soup. Hamilton sat with his hands palms down on the table. His drink was between them. He moved as though to pick up the glass but his hand faltered and returned to its place. His gaze was fixed over Crawford's shoulder. Crawford swallowed his drink and set the glass down with a neat tap. He looked around for the waitress. When he was sure she had taken note of his glance, he looked at Hamilton and observed he had not changed the direction of his gaze. Turning, he saw a travel poster on the wall behind him, dim behind its glass, which sought to enhance its exhortation to visit Italy with a scene from some ancient story involving a broken column, nymphs, and a wood in whose shadows a dark pool gleamed. The White Rock girl, was it? thought Crawford, and then reflected that it looked a lot more like the White Rock boy. The confusion was apt, he thought, under the circumstances. But Hamilton, he saw, was not really looking at this picture at all, he was not looking at anything, not seeing anything. Understandable, thought Crawford. Christ, he said to himself. But aloud he only said, "Hey. Hey, drink your drink." Then he repeated, "How does liver and onions strike you?"

Hamilton looked at him. "Yes," he said.

"Drink up then," said Crawford, as the waitress put before him his second martini. She drew a pad and pencil from her apron pocket and asked if they were ready to order.

"Yes, indeedy," said the doctor. "I will have liver and onions, please. And my friend, I believe, will have the same. Do you think you can arrange that?"

"Medium?" she asked.

"Rare," said Crawford.

"Peas or green beans?" she said. "It comes with it."

"No," said Crawford, "nothing. Just tell him to put on a little extra onions, like a good girl."

"Okey-doke," she said, returning her pad to her pocket. Crawford observed her short stiff uniform twitch over her buttocks as she retreated. "Very neat," he said to Hamilton and then fell silent, struck by the inappropriateness, under the circumstances, of the remark.

Nothing seemed quite appropriate, however. As a rule, they talked about women, sports, politics, money. Hamilton had represented Crawford in a malpractice suit that was settled out of court. He had handled both his divorces and after the second had sold the Westport house for him. At one time they had invested in soft lenses together, and together they had lost a little money in California varietals. He had given Hamilton his checkups, sent him to Sperry for his tennis elbow, and gone over himself one night with morphine and a syringe to help ease the passing of a kidney stone. Just out of college, they had traveled together in Spain, and twice when they were both married at the same time they had gone with their wives to the Caribbean, once to Antigua and once to St. Kitts. But at this moment, neither investments nor vacations seemed suitable topics.

"Feldman is a good man," said Crawford.

Hamilton said nothing. He looked, to Crawford, as though he was made of wax. I have to get out of here, thought the doctor.

"Think of it as a growth. Why not think of it as merely a growth?" he said. "Let Feldman take care of it."

The waitress put down their full plates.

"Nice and rare," said Crawford, examining the square of meat on his fork. Chewing, he watched Hamilton pick up his knife and fork and slowly slice off a small piece of liver. Red bubbles rose at the cut. His knife and fork fell to the table as Hamilton stood up with a white face and stumbled toward the corridor behind the kitchen. Crawford rose to follow him and found him, as he expected he would, retching, with one hand on the knob of a door marked "Gents" and ornamented with a painted top hat between two black eighth notes. Bilious foam was gently sliding on the uneven floor. Hamilton, gasping, was bent over. He turned his eyes up at the doctor. "God," he said.

The waitress appeared in the doorway. "Uh-oh," she said.

Crawford reached for his wallet. "Here you go," he said, giving her a ten-dollar bill. "Sorry about this."

"Oh, listen," she said. "Luis does it."

"That's OK," said Crawford. "You can split it with him."

Hamilton stood upright. At Crawford's suggestion, he drank a sip of water.

Out on the street, he refused Doug's offer to drop him off at home on his way to the hospital and got into a cab, saying he was going to the office.

"Sure?" said Crawford. Hamilton said he was sure.

"Keep in touch," said Crawford. "Fella," he added, after a fractional pause.

Hamilton sat back in the seat, but just before the cab turned to get on the Drive, he leaned forward and instructed the driver to take him home. He rested his head against the upholstery and closed his eyes.

When Charles got home he felt quite well. He sat down in the living room to think. Then he stood up and thoughtfully shook some fish food on the surface of the water and watched the fish rise to feed. It was unusual for him to be home on a weekday afternoon, and the silence of the apartment, the dark afternoon light, and the still, heated air combined to arouse in him a quite unusual sadness and anxiety. He kept forgetting and remembering why it was he was at home. The fish were all at the top of the tank, nosing for a last bite. He resisted the temptation to give them more, a little dessert. He thought he might take the car out. He thought it might be a good idea to drive out to the ocean and walk on the beach to clear his mind. What course was open to him? What choices did he have? As was his custom, he reached for a yellow pad and a pencil and wrote: *Options*. Then he underlined the word "options" and below he wrote a figure one. After the "1" he made a dot and then circled the dot. Then he put the pad down on the glass coffee table. At least I'm not sick, he thought, but the relief he invoked refused to come. Instead he was filled with dread and despair. He let his hands open, and the pencil fell to the floor. His eyes closed and his mouth hung open. He gave a long sigh. He was not sick, though. That was something to be grateful for. He yawned painfully. He heard the rain. He fell asleep in the chair.

When he woke, it was dark. He had dreamed he was in the car, near the shore. It was his own car, the BMW, he was quite sure of that, but he had not been driving. Who the driver was he didn't know, because the whole time he had been looking out the window at scenes of astonishing beauty. He had seen a bay ringed around with black trees. The water of the bay was streaked with gold. At the far end it opened to the ocean, which was itself entirely golden.

With a dry mouth he stumbled to his bed, where he dreamed another dream, this time of Simon Rutherford, who approached him in the office corridor with a knife. To defend himself he had grasped Simon by the wrist and stood with feet apart, calling upon all his strength to hold the knife away from his body. Simon's arm and his own slowly descended as Simon, who in the dream was possessed of a strength incommensurate with his age, gained in the struggle until Charles, seeing that he was about to lose, began to look wildly about for another way out of his predicament. In the distance he saw a grove of trees and a stream of bright water where a small child was standing with a dazzled expression. To keep Simon from seeing the child he forced him with great effort to turn and then with a sharp thrust pushed against him with his head and ducked under his extended arm. But having freed himself, he woke and gazed wildly around his dark bedroom looking for the light-struck spot where the child was standing.

He got up to get a glass of water. The rain was over. Below, the wet streets shone. It was nearly morning.

He sat on the edge of the bed. Who is Charles Hamilton, he thought, that this should happen to him? Was it a punishment? If so, what was he being punished for?

In kindergarten, he recalled, he had stolen two dolls. He

had hidden them under his jacket in the cloakroom until the children were dismissed. After school he had succeeded in spiriting them out of the building and the schoolyard, escaping the notice of the other children. A thief of dolls, he bent over as he ran, with his jacket wrapped around them and his lunch box banging against his knees. He tumbled down the gully at the edge of the playground overgrown with dread sumac, purple asters, and the flat, hairy-leafed plant the children called elephant weed. Huddled there, he waited, as he had planned, until the shouts and calls of the children gave way to an exciting silence broken only by the rustling of leaves and the sound of falling pebbles dislodged by his tensely planted feet. When he was confident of privacy, or as confident as he was going to be, accepting, as he did, the risk that some straggler could always peer down and see him among the weeds and bushes, he uncovered the dolls. Sitting down on the ground, he put one doll in his lunch box to await her turn. The other he took in his hands. She had large round blue eyes, but not the kind that opened and shut, and round full cheeks. Her lips were parted slightly to show her teeth. He tilted her head back the better to see inside her mouth, but it was an illusion; you could not really see inside. She was made of something smooth and hard but with a little springiness to it as well. She was not as soft as a person, but not as hard as wood. Her head was quite a lot harder than her body. And she didn't have real hair. Instead, her hair was suggested by a series of raised curves around her face, which were colored light brown and which smoothed out as they got farther back from her face. She was made of seven pieces: head, neck, body, arms, and legs. He counted them to be sure, carefully raising up her short dress. Her legs were round and fat, as were her feet, and they were slightly bent in a position that would make it quite impossible for her to stand up. She wasn't supposed to stand up anyway. She was a baby.

The other doll, although smaller, was not a baby. She

was a little girl. She had neat flat feet, and he knew at a glance she could be got to stand up, although not here in the gully where there wasn't anything flat to stand her on. She had real hair. She was not soft; in fact, she was hard, but she did have tiny fascinating features: lips, eyelashes, nostrils. Each finger was separate.

Holding both dolls steady by their outer arms, he stood them on his knees and looked at them together. Who do you like best? he asked himself. Observing that the baby's cheeks were dirty, he cleaned them with spit and dried them with the edge of his shirt. He kissed her on her clean cheek, gently, as if she was his baby sister. Then he kissed the little girl doll in her turn. The game, if it was a game, was over. There was no more to be done with them. He was unsatisfied. They were only dolls and he was a boy. He had thought he could play with them, he had thought it would be fun to play with them, but it wasn't.

Often, stopping with a block in each hand, seeing the girls feverishly washing, tucking, diapering in the doll corner, he felt a tugging desire to watch, or even perhaps to rub a washcloth on a doll's cheek, or press a spoon against a resistant mouth, saying as severely as a girl, "Now you eat this all up." But even though one or two boys did play with the dolls, he could not, except as now, by stealth. But he had not been able to steal, along with the dolls, the red-cheeked bustle of the doll corner where the girls shook the doll carriages to send their babies to sleep with movements so energetic they were often tossed back under the hood.

Grown Charles recalled how small Charles had mounted the steep slope of the gully, leaving the stolen dolls behind, stuffed in a crack between two rocks and covered over with handfuls of leaves torn from the elephant plant. He had intended, he had fully intended, to go back the next morning before school and, having disinterred the two, to return them unseen to the shelf in the doll corner. He did not do it that morning, although he thought he surely would the next. But he didn't do it the next morning either. Instead, he entered the playground from the other side and thereafter kept far away from the gully. After a time he quite forgot why it was he had changed his route to and from school.

This predicament then, this monstrous problem, could be thought of as a punishment, true, but what was to be gained by thinking of it thus? Nothing. Charles, seated on the edge of his bed, turned his head and saw the red edge of the sun appear above a warehouse in Queens. Quickly, reddish light spilled over the roofs and down the walls of the buildings and slid to the gray river. Salmon, rose, and orange, all the colors of the family of red, swam to the Manhattan side. He stood up to watch. It lasted only a minute, the flaring of pink, before it was replaced by blue and yellow, black and white, the ordinary colors of morning. Perhaps, thought Charles, he was not being punished for anything at all. Perhaps it should be seen in some other way altogether.

It was day. Retrieving from the living room the yellow pad and pencil that had dropped from his hands the evening before, he began to make a new list. First he wrote *Call Feldman* and then *Call office,* which was needless, since he would call the office without reminding himself to have Karen cancel his appointments. He was going to have to tell her to cancel more than today's appointments, but he would get around to telling her that in due time. The firm, since Simon's death, was in some disarray over the question of succession. It was no time to be away. But away he was going to have to be. The question was, would he be away for a long time or a short? If Haroun was right about the "trimester" and he was going to see the thing to the end, then—here he began to count on his fingers—then he was going to be out of commission, as he put it to himself, until September, at least. Longer. There probably wasn't any way of shaving these things. But why not think of it, as Doug had proposed, as merely a growth, a tumor? In

that case, he would be back in the saddle by Easter or
shortly thereafter, the whole issue a thing of the past, forgotten. He shuddered, recalling the dream in which he had
been struggling with old Simon, and for an instant felt
again the urgency of that struggle. As dreams go, it had
been uncannily real.

He dialed Feldman's office but it was still too early. The
answering service put him on hold. After a minute, the
girl inquired whether or not it was an emergency. She said
the word "emergency" in an interesting way, and Charles
imagined the voice of an anxious husband calling the doctor before office hours, anxious because something either
timely or untimely was happening during the early hours.
As, folklore had it, it often did. Charles said to the girl—
black, clearly—that it was not an emergency and she instructed him to call after nine, when he would be connected
with the office. Hoping to catch him at home, he called
Doug but only got his machine, which said, in Doug's
voice, that he could not speak to him at this time, but if
he would leave his name, number, and a brief message
after the beep, his call would be returned as soon as possible. To his friend, or his friend's machine, rather, he said
it was him, Charley, and would he call him back at home,
where he expected to be the whole day.

Hungry, and with good reason, he thought, since he had
slept straight through dinnertime and to all practical pur-
poses had eaten nothing at lunch, he briskly made for the
refrigerator and stood with one hand on the open door,
the other against the frame, bending his head toward its
disappointing contents. He had always been amused with
himself, and pleased, too, that his refrigerator, like that of
Doug and other men of his acquaintance, was, in essence,
empty. There were, of course, exceptional moments before
a party when it burst with pâté, Explorateur, smoked fish;
after the party, he would pick for days at the drying remains
until Gloria, his seldom-seen cleaning woman, decided that
it was time enough and cleaned out the whole lot, leaving

the familiar bright shelves empty except for grapefruit juice and cocktail onions. Almost invariably, he had breakfast in the office and at home had no more than a cup of instant coffee, standing up. But in the freezer he found English muffins and butter, and in the cupboard dark jam, interesting looking, and in due time he sat down to breakfast. The jam, especially, was delicious.

Later, he made an appointment with Dr. Feldman for that afternoon. This he managed to do with some difficulty. Doug, it seemed, had not called Feldman as he had promised he would, and the girl sounded uncooperative and said the soonest appointment she could give him would not be until May, but suddenly she relented and told him there had been a cancellation and he could come in that afternoon at three. "Dr. Crawford referred you?" she asked.

"**D**r. Crawford referred you?" asked Eugene Feldman, looking at him through horn-rimmed glasses. He had red lips and a small black mustache.

"Yes," said Charles. "He said you were a good man."

"Ah," said the doctor, swiveling back and forth on his desk chair, which squeaked softly under him. "And your problem is...?"

But Charles stood up. He had let Doug take blood from his veins and listen to the hums and thumps of his body. He had urinated for him as he had for Dr. Haroun. He had docilely lain down for Haroun's girl and had stayed still while they did their greasy business. At Doug's command he had trotted obediently to the radiologist and would have done whatever was required of him there, had not the radiologist's girl, at Doug's instructions, sent him running back. Not that he blamed Doug, although he noted that he had not returned his call. But he had to find some other way to pull himself out of this tangle. Help he needed, that was sure. There was no way he could manage alone, but nonetheless he found he could not tell this man what

34

it was he had come for. He stood on the balls of his feet, looking fiercely around. His eyes swept the bookshelves, the diplomas, the colored engravings. Uncertainty yawned on all sides. "Aahh," he gasped, and it seemed to him he heard a great crack.

"I believe," he said in a voice that sounded strong to him, surprisingly strong, "I believe I have come to the wrong place."

And he walked out, right out to the street, easy as that.

In the following days, Charles saw, or made appointments to see, an assortment of physicians: one, clearly an addict, in Yonkers; two in Brooklyn; two in Queens, in Long Island City and in Corona; and three in Manhattan, in Washington Heights, in Harlem, and on Canal Street. This last, a young woman, seemed hardly in his opinion to be a physician at all, or to have ever been one, rather, since none of those he had seen corresponded to his idea of a proper doctor, shabby as they were, or dirty, or seemingly addicted to one thing or another. The young woman received him in a lavender garment that left her waist bare, causing him to look to see if she was an Indian, which to his way of thinking would have made it all right. He saw her fair skin and pale blue eyes.

"Did you ever hear of a man having a baby?" he asked.

"Far out," she said, lighting a stick of incense and attempting with little success to set it upright in a brass saucer. "Oh, there."

The smell of the thing began to invade the room. How unpleasant it was!

"Hey, wait a minute," she said, turning so that her light blue skirt swirled around her ankles, her dirty ankles, Charles observed. "What'm I saying? Anything could happen, right?"

"Right," said Charles.

The light from the window was dim, making its way

through the dusty panes and a thick screen of dust-bearing leaves of the climbing plants that sought the ceiling from a row of large pots on the floor.

"Sit down, if you want," she said. "I'll be with you in a minute." Noteworthy that even in this grimy place advertised as the offices of Dr. Jeannie, Herbal Medicines, the formula was the familiar "Have a seat. Doctor will see you soon." Was this dirty child the doctor? Charles looked about for a chair. Seeing none, he remained standing.

"Go ahead," she called out to him, "sit down." He spread the pages of the *Voice,* the source of the advertisement which had brought him here, and sat down on the splintery floor. Presently she appeared and sat facing him, spreading her voluminous skirt over her crossed legs. She sat with a good deal more ease in this position, the lotus position, he believed it was, than he.

"OK," she said. "What do you want? Massage? Shiatsu? What?"

"What do you do?"

She gave him a smile, a crooked smile. He understood that she was telling him she would fill whatever prescription he gave her. From the street he heard the rumble of heavy traffic.

He put his palms on the floor to help himself stand up.

"Hey," she said, her smile gone. "Who are you? Are you a cop or something? Are you from the paper?"

"No," said Charles, brushing the dust from his knees. "Not those. I just wanted some herbs, but I think I am in the wrong place."

Home, done with the search, sickened by those tawdry offices, Charles fell backward on his bed, but the sight of his swollen abdomen reminded him that he could not be done. Even though he had decided—or, rather, in some way he could not account for, it had been decided for him—that he was to see this thing, bizarre as it was, through to the end, there was no way out of his predicament without engaging the assistance of some kind of medico, Jew,

Greek, or what-have-you. It was now May. "Just tell them
I'm having a nervous breakdown," he had said to Peter
Woods, who called from the office every morning
throughout April. It was a while since Peter had called.
Doug he had not spoken to again since the liver lunch. He
had not spoken to anyone, the fact was, save for these
assorted quasi-physicians and their receptionists. More
likely their wives, or girlfriends, or whatever. Not true;
he had talked to cabdrivers, waitresses, the elevator man,
and Gloria, his usually unseen cleaning lady. But Gloria
was no longer unseen. Since he now stayed at home, he
saw her regularly, on Tuesdays and Fridays. Today was
Tuesday; she was vacuuming in the hall. He heard the thing
humming and growling. He got up to close the bedroom
door, but with one hand on the door handle he found
himself eye to eye with Gloria, who, over the din of the
machine, was asking him could she bring him some lunch,
looking, as he did, "peaky."

All these weeks Charles had been pretending to Gloria
that he was not staying home and only venturing out occasionally, in his raincoat, whatever the weather, but was
going about his normal life and that the fact that they met
biweekly and spoke face to face instead of by notes left on
the counter in front of the toaster, hers printed and his
scrawled, was merely an odd series of circumstantially produced coincidences.

"Should I bring you something for your lunch?" she
asked again. "I could bring it on a tray and you could get
into your bed, which I done made already."

This suggestion and the tone in which it was made, as
well, perhaps, as the tender solicitous look that accompanied it, produced in Charles an unexpected reaction.
Tears started in his eyes, a constriction seized his throat,
sobs rose in his chest. He retreated to his bedroom and sat
down on the bed. Holding his fists against his eyes, he
cried loudly, with moans and prolonged sobs. Gloria, in
the hall, hastened to silence the vacuum cleaner and having

done so rushed to sit beside him. "There," she said, "you ain't feeling right. I can see that." She put her arms around him. Charles, despite his gasps and the shaking of his body, hesitated for an instant, this being so unlikely an event, before he relaxed and rested against her soft, scented, generous person. Gradually, the force and frequency of his spasms lessened and his sobs were gently reduced from the painfully forced to an easy rhythmic snuffling, interrupted by an occasional hiccough. The relaxation he felt was so extreme, so unaccustomed, and so pleasant that he was loath to sit up and breathe normally, even when no more sobs pressed their way from his chest. His eyes were closed. He felt as though he was lying down in a little boat that trembled slightly on the surface of an almost still pond. Gloria was patting him gently on the shoulder. "Lamb," she said. He drew away.

He sighed.

"Gloria," he said, and raised his eyes to her face.

She was looking at him intently. "You having your changes?" she asked. "Mr. Hamilton, what is wrong with you?"

"I have to find a doctor," he said.

"You do have to find a doctor. Something *is* wrong with you. What kind of doctor you looking for?"

"A—" He hesitated, then looked at her slyly. "A woman's doctor."

"A gynecologist?" Gloria looked puzzled, then smiled widely. "Mr. Hamilton, never in my days. I ain't never seen no man so broke up 'cause he done got some—" She broke off. "Is that what is tormenting you? You are surely some kind of a saint."

"No, no," said Charles, "not that. It's not that. I need a doctor who will..."

Gloria, it seemed, had a recommendation to make. In her building, uptown, there was an old man, a very old man, who had doctored her and her long-grown children, her neighbors, many people she knew. He had eased her mother's passing, years ago, and, more recently, her husband's. Nowadays, she said, he did no doctoring. He never went out. Nobody in the neighborhood knew him any more. Gloria took down his scanty garbage with hers, did his small shopping for him, and on Sundays brought him over a piece of chicken or a few ribs. If Charles would come uptown with her this evening, when she had finished her work, she would take him to see the doctor. She said that she could not vouch for his acquaintance with the newer methods. Probably, she said, he was still living in the olden days, medicine-wise, but she, for one, believed in him. "He can't hurt you," she said, "and maybe he can help you, whatever is wrong with you."

She returned to her vacuuming and Charles lay down on his bed to wait. He heard the water run in the bathtub, then in the kitchen. The dishwasher started. The refrigerator door opened and closed. Footsteps. Sighs. Little knocks and thumps. Different soapy and waxy smells reached him. Then, for a while, there was silence.

At length, Gloria appeared in the doorway, dressed to go home.

"You coming?" she asked. Charles rose to follow her.

The doctor was indeed old: eighty, ninety, Charles could not say. He was a small man, tiny, with fine white hair, in a dark creased suit, a white shirt, and a thin, wrinkled black tie. His sleeves hung below his hands, from one of which dangled his eyeglasses. Behind him, the room, up too many flights for someone so old, was oddly spare: no photographs, no little objects.

He smiled at Gloria. "Thank you, Mrs. White," he said, "for bringing me a patient. I will do for him the best I can." He had a curious way of speaking, Charles noticed, despite his agitation, hard to pinpoint. Foreign.

"Good evening, Doctor. So long, Mr. Hamilton," said Gloria. "See you Friday. Good luck."

When Gloria had closed the door, the old man turned to Charles. "My name is Dr. Weiss," he said. He put on his wire glasses. "Tell me what is your trouble."

It was dark when Charles walked out of the building, descended the stoop, and started home. What the old man had promised him was miraculous, too good to be true. He would take care of him. In June, in less than a month, he, Charles, would come and get the old man in his car. The doctor had asked if he had a car. He would pick him up and drive them to a little house the old man had far out on Long Island. Where on the Island? Charles had asked. Near where the tail divides, the doctor had answered. What does he mean, Riverhead? thought Charles, but he didn't ask. The old man seemed to relish not saying exactly where. He had had this house for many years, he said, but it was many years since he had seen it, many, because he had no way to get there, no one to help him take down the shutters or prime the pump. It is lovely at my house, he had said, and Charles noticed there was something interesting in the way he said "lovely." There, the doctor said, they would pass the summer, plant some vegetables, and look at the sky from the porch. And there, at the end of the summer, when the time was right, he would be able to do for Charles, and the child, whatever was necessary. "I will be glad to see my house one more time," he said as Charles thanked him.

Charles had his hand on the doorknob, about to leave, when he turned around and asked in a voice that struck him as childish and weak a question he longed to ask. "Has this ever happened to anyone else?" he said.

But the old man, seeming not to have heard, called out that it was the first of June they had agreed upon, he would be downstairs on the sidewalk at twelve o'clock sharp, they would plant cucumbers, they would hear the birds.

In June, then, on the agreed-upon day, Charles took the car out of the garage and told Jenkins, the attendant, that that was it for a while; he would be away for the summer. He gave him twenty-five dollars and they shook hands. Jenkins wished him a good summer, and just before Charles accelerated up the ramp, he gave the car a couple of pats on the rear fender, as though to wish him, and it, on their way.

The sky was blue and clear. The river on his right glittered; what he knew was far looked near. On Riker's Island the lawns were green. Now and then the fumes of the highway were pierced by the smell of something sweetly blossoming, causing Charles to inhale deeply and turn his nose to the open window. As had been true these last months, Charles continued to alternately forget and remember what lay ahead; nevertheless, in the back of his mind, something shadowy and large was always there. He had, at least in an immediate sense, put his affairs in order. Gloria had received her instructions, as had Connally, the superintendent. To the office he had given a *Poste Restante* address in Paris and had got a friend from law school now practicing in Paris to agree to return the mail to his apartment, whence Gloria would send it on to Suffolk County, when so instructed. How he would rebuild his reputation for reliability he would tend to later, when he returned.

Although the old man had said he would be downstairs waiting with his things when Charles arrived, he was not. Charles drove around the block twice, slowly. Finally he parked between an iridescent Pontiac and the shell of a green Chevy. He left the car with some anxiety, irritated with the old man for making him have to do just what he had foreseen and thought he had avoided by careful planning. He had even telephoned just before he left home. He walked up the flaking pink stoop. In the hall, between two adolescents of the sort he referred to as "youths," he rang the doctor's bell.

Ready at last, the old man tottered to the car. He blinked

41

in the sunlight. Dressed in a linen suit, yellow, which looked as if it might have once been white, he waited for Charles to open the door. He got in and folded his hands. Charles slammed the door and walked around to the other side, checking for scratches. As he got into the car, Charles, who was wearing a loose yellow linen shirt himself, once a favorite, now a necessity, observed the similarity, but it was the old man who held his sleeve against Charles's as if to say, See?

At first, as they drove, the old man looked this way and that, but soon he fell asleep. His slight body wobbled from side to side. Charles wished he had got him to fasten the seat belt. Under the pretext of needing gas, he turned off the expressway. Before they started again, he reached across and fastened the belt for the old man, who fumbled with it and then shrugged. But it was hardly better; even neatly belted in, as soon as he was asleep again, the old man drooped and began to slide on the leather seat. It was a bad omen to be at the mercy of so insubstantial a frame.

"What exit?" said Charles loudly. "Why don't you tell me exactly where we're going? And then you can just sleep."

"Go on, go on," said the old man in a peremptory voice, waving his hand in front of his face as though to dispose of some flying creature. "I'll tell you when."

"Is it the North Fork? You must give me a general idea. Should I go as far as Riverhead?"

But the old man made the same gesture, which seemed at once to brush away both the question and Charles himself.

"Just drive," he said. "I'll tell you."

Silent but vastly irritated, Charles drove. It was a familiar route with spots where the traffic jammed and stuck in a way well-known to Charles from many a summer weekend, but, it being the middle of the day in the middle of the week, after a while the traffic thinned. With his dozing passenger sliding from one side to the other beside him, he let his foot down on the accelerator and felt the power of the car. Displeased with his role as chauffeur, it seemed to him that by driving faster he gained some ascendency over the old man. No doubt they would get lost. He hoped so.

"Here," said the old man, suddenly opening his eyes, and Charles, muttering, "For God's sake," was forced to swerve from the fast lane so as not to miss the exit.

"I think you drive too fast," said the doctor.

"You didn't give me any warning. I told you to tell me where we were going."

"In addition," said the doctor, "you shouldn't take the Lord's name in vain."

"Right," said Charles. He would deposit the old bugger at his doorstep, wherever it was, set his cartons and black suitcase tied with string in front of the house, and turn straight back to New York. But at that thought, the reason he was driving this crotchety old man to the outback of Suffolk County presented itself in full force. He was not free to leave. He was tied to him until September. They were tied to each other by the agreement they'd made. He would deliver the doctor, together with his boxes and whatnot, help him put up the screens, and do whatever was needed to open the house; in short, he would be houseboy to the old man, who, in turn, would be midwife to him.

"Now," said the doctor, "turn. Take the next right." He was sitting forward in his seat in expectation. Charles glanced at him and saw that he was getting ready for the sight of his long-unseen little house, which, he had told Charles that evening in his apartment in Harlem, had been left to him by an old lady he had taken care of long ago, twenty or maybe thirty years ago, when he was able to manage better than now. Now, his arms were folded over his chest, his chin was lifted, and his eyebrows raised. On his lips was a little smile. He turned his head from side to side. My little house, he seemed to be saying, where are you, my little house?

Charles was filled with rage and despair. He made the turn so sharply that the old man was thrown against him. He felt his pointy chin dig into his arm. Charles slowed at once. "Sorry," he said.

"Almost there," said the doctor, righting himself by pushing with the flat of his hand against Charles's arm. "Ha!" he said. Then he said, "No-o-o," shaking his head, and then "Ha!" again. Charles drove looking straight ahead with a leaden heart. The last thing he had expected, after the relief of finding him, was that he would be enraged by the old man. The idea that he had found a way through his problem and a place to conceal himself until it was over had imparted to the months ahead a pleasant glow. Although he was not aware of his precise expectations, he had dimly pictured himself lying in a rattan garden chair dressed in a sort of a burnoose, on the veranda of a big shingled summer house with turrets. He was reading, and on a little rattan table comfortably at hand was a glass down whose cool sides rolled beads of moisture. He turned a page. The whole thing could well be an opportunity to read Plutarch, or Dante, or even Spinoza; it could be a chance to think. And in this picturing he had done, the doctor had been a benign minor figure in the background, an elderly retainer, not exactly a butler because of his vague but necessary medical aura but someone in the wings alert to bring to him whatever it was he needed. He had not imagined he would have to contend with a peremptory ancient who saw himself as the interesting character and Charles as someone who could be dismissed with a wave of the hand. And there was nothing to do, thought Charles, but wait it out.

"Here," sang out the doctor in a singsong, giving the word two syllables.

Charles turned off the blacktop onto a dirt road, making

the turn cautiously. Tall grass brushed the flanks of the car. "We're here because we're here because we're here because we're here," sang the old man. He leaned toward Charles and said in a friendly way, "I learned that when I came first to this country, when I was a camp doctor. A children's camp." Charles continued to drive carefully past shrubs and brambles, which made distressing noises as he eased the car by. "Here," said the doctor. "Charles," he said, using his name for the first time, "stop. We're here."

At the sight of the house—the shack, rather, or so it seemed at first glance—every trace of Charles's picture of himself reading the books he had never got to in college and drinking weak Scotch and soda vanished. The dirt road had tapered off some distance away from what you might call a cottage, but which was so heavily overgrown that little of it was visible. Vines grew up over the roof and down to the ground. When a breeze fluttered the leaves, you could see the glint of a window. The way the twisting vines sagged forward from the roof suggested a porch beneath, but nothing of a porch could be seen, nor of steps leading up to it, nor of a door leading inside.

The doctor had got out of the car and was looking toward the house. Brambles higher than his head barred the way. With one white hand he was trying to push aside a thorny spur.

"Well," said Charles with a certain malicious pleasure, "how long did you say it was since you were last here?"

"It is all right. We will fix it up. You will fix it up for us."

"I?" said Charles.

By nightfall Charles was sitting at the kitchen table with raw hands. He had ripped a path through the blackberry and pulled wisteria and honeysuckle from the porch. Dots of dried blood tracked his arms. He looked at his hands. The doctor was dabbing at them with a wad of cotton, which he had dipped into a cool clear liquid in a saucer. The liquid had a pungent, unpleasant odor that Charles inhaled with dim pleasure. He couldn't think of its name, but it carried with it some childish association.

While he was hacking at roots and tearing the vines away from the house, the old man had called him from the door of the toolshed to help pull from its moldy depths a tricycle, of a size suitable to a nearly grown child, upon which he proposed to pedal to the village to shop for provisions. He remembered the way perfectly, he said. Charles stood watching the tricycle bump off down the sandy track. When it was out of sight, he turned back to his slashing. Bees flew out of blossoms. Pollen fell on his head. Sweat was running into his eyes, and his wet shirt stuck to his belly.

By the time the doctor returned with the tricycle's wire basket full of paper bags, the sun had set. Charles was sitting on the top step of the porch in a cloud of mosquitoes looking with bitter satisfaction at his bloody hands.

The doctor patted them gently with the wet cotton. Charles watched him wind long strips of gauze around first one hand and then the other, tying the end neatly around his wrist, leaving him mittened, with two white paws.

"There," said the doctor. "That is better. That is good."

"OK," said Charles. "Thanks. But I don't know why we didn't get somebody to do that for us."

"For us," said the doctor.

Charles looked at him sharply, but he was putting away his scissors and gauze. Overhead, moths fluttered against the kerosene lamp that hung from a crossbeam above the table.

"All right," said the doctor, fastening his bag. "Now we will have our supper. You rest."

Charles sat, feeling his hands throb under the bandages, while the doctor lifted cans and boxes out of the paper bags. A mosquito whined at his ear, and he tried to kill it by pressing it between his wrist and his head. He feared to try to hit it hard lest he further injure his hand. The mosquito bit him on the back of the neck.

The old man took two bowls from the shelf, rubbed them against his shirt, then, upon inspecting them, seemed to find them insufficiently clean. He ran water over them at the sink. The light in the room was dim. Except for the vines that grew over them, there were no screens at the windows, pale dust lay upon everything, and looking down the hall from the kitchen, Charles could see that books lay in disorder on the floor, knocked down by mice or fallen themselves, water-soaked from years of autumn storms. It occurred to him that he could drive with his elbows and get to a motel, lie on the bed, look at television, and get out of this. The doctor set on the table two bowls of cornflakes, put milk and sugar in one, sat down, and began to eat with enthusiasm. Charles, watching him, thought, I wonder when he's going to notice I can't pick up the spoon, but said nothing. The doctor finished the bowl and got up to get more. He sat down and began to eat again. He ate with considerable noise. Charles was glad.

After a while, however, Charles said, in a voice he did not recognize, "I can't eat."

The old man looked up from his bowl.

"I can't even hold the spoon."

"Oh, I see," said the old man, setting his milky spoon down on the table. "Come," he said, "I will feed you." Moving his chair away, he stood close to Charles and poured first milk, then sugar, into his bowl. Charles was seized by the sudden thought of knocking the cereal to the floor, but instead, seeing the spoon at his lips, he opened his mouth. He swallowed, tasting the milk, feeling the grains of sugar against his teeth, and opened his mouth again. Another spoonful was waiting.

"There," said the doctor.

Charles looked up into the old man's face. He was watching Charles's mouth, intent upon bringing the spoon to

47

the right place at the right time. At the same time, in the ancient fashion of those who feed babies, his own lips were parted as though they expected the spoonful for themselves.

At this moment, Charles, whether from fatigue or the frustration of being unable to feed himself, or for some other reason unknown to him, began to cry. The doctor put down the bowl and looked into the weeping man's face. He extended one hand to pat his shoulder, but when Charles twisted away, he took the two bowls to the sink. Then he came back to the table and sat down. Charles's sobs passed, he stopped shaking. At length he was done crying.

"I hate this place," he said.

The moths bumped against the globe. Water dripped into the sink. The lamp swung a little and the light dimmed, then brightened. A powerful odor of honeysuckle entered the window, and in the distance dogs barked, here, there, and farther away. A breeze started up and the honeysuckle at the window was pushed inside and then, as by a breath, drawn out. Charles gave a shaky sigh. He was feeling the great ease that follows tears. He looked at the doctor and gave a small shrug.

"Yah," said the doctor. "You were tired. And the strain. And also the hands. I am sorry about your hands. I cannot do what you did to clear. I am too old." He wiped Charles's eyes with the edge of a damp paper napkin. Charles lifted his face to received the pats. "You should go to sleep now," said the doctor.

"I want my cornflakes before I go to bed," said Charles, now hungry.

And so it was that he sat opening his mouth and swallowing, while the doctor fed him one spoonful after another and, between spoonfuls, patted the milk from his lips. Charles said nothing while he ate. His eyes roved around the room. He saw the dishes on the shelves, the cups hanging on hooks below, the cream-colored enamel

stove on legs with the name *Vulcan* written in flowing
letters on the oven door, from which the black handle hung
loose, fastened only at one end. On the floor he saw the
light green and yellow squares of the linoleum, each square
marbled, the yellow with light green, the light green with
yellow. In one corner of the room the linoleum had come
loose and was standing up a little. Charles turned his head
to see if it was like that in the other corners.

"Finished? Are you finished?" asked the doctor.

"Yes," said Charles. "All finished." He raised his bandaged paws so as not to bump them as he stood up. "Thank
you for feeding me," he said. "Where's my room? Which
is my room?"

His room, it turned out, was not in disorder. It was a
small narrow room with a bed against the wall under the
window, an iron washstand, and on the floor a white ceramic pot. Charles sat down on the bed.

"Can you manage by yourself?" asked the doctor, who
had set Charles's mocha carry-on bag on the floor. "Or
perhaps—" He gestured to indicate that he would assist
him with the unfastening of his belt.

"I can do it," said Charles in a fretful voice.

"Very good, then," said the doctor with one hand on
the door. "Sleep well." He closed the door.

Charles heard the old man's footsteps in the hall.

"Doctor!" he called. "Doctor!"

He heard the footsteps coming back.

"Yes?" asked the doctor, opening the door. "What do
you want?"

"I want you to leave the door open."

"Like this?"

"Yes," said Charles and was shortly asleep.

He dreamed no story, only scenes. He saw spinning past
him trays of glittering objects, blue and red, lovely. Once
he woke up. Strangely enough, he knew exactly where he
was. He heard the old man singing in a droning voice. He
was pushing something, or pulling something, in another

part of the house. Charles fell back to sleep, hoping to see those twinkling things again.

In the morning, when the sun struck the side of the house, Charles opened his eyes. For a long time he lay gazing at the window shade, which although water-stained and cracked was rendered orange and glowing by the strong early light. He could see the thin strip of wood in the hem of the shade. The hem was secured with cross-stitching, a bit of which had come undone, letting one corner of the fabric curl stiffly. The sunlight penetrated the holes through which the hemming thread had passed, and although ordinarily these holes would have been imperceptible the intensity of the light made them look like little stars. With difficulty he sat up in bed to examine them closely. His hands, he noticed, were bandaged. He must have hurt them. He could not remember how. The end of the bandage on his right hand hung loose. Holding it in his teeth, by twisting his wrist and bobbing his head, he unwound it and then, with the help of his free hand, unwound the other. There was nothing wrong with his hands at all. They were all better. Witch hazel, he thought, remembering the doctor patting them with the wet cotton.

Fingering the shade, he noticed it was both crackly and fuzzy. The string pull was gone. The hole through which it had been fastened was like a little sun. He knelt on the bed to peek through the hole so he could see into the garden, but the sun flamed in his eye. He pulled back his head and tried to raise the shade, but it refused to respond to his gentle tug, the spring having given way long ago. Standing unsteadily on the bed, he extracted the shade from its holder by first lifting it out of the bucket with the square slot and then retracting it from the round hole in the bucket on the other side. Steadying himself with both hands on the window frame, he stood looking out. Outside, a long meadow glistened in the sun. The heads of the meadow grass were just ripe enough to begin to bend toward the earth. Yellow and white butterflies rose and sank, and here and there yellow flowers were blooming. A steady breeze kept everything in motion: grasses, flowers, butterflies, and the honeysuckle that was rubbing against the window. In the meadow, the doctor was walking with uncertain steps. His shirt fluttered about his slender body, and his hair, lit by the sun behind him, shone silver. Pressing his face against the glass, Charles waved, but the old man did not look up.

The beauty of the meadow and the sight of the fragile old man passing dreamily through it combined to inspire in Charles a sudden happiness. He rapped on the window and the doctor stopped, turned toward him, squinted, and waved.

Eager to go outside, Charles lowered himself carefully to a sitting position and stood up. Under his weight his feet spread. He pulled the shirt he had slept in close to him to look at his feet. They looked quite as usual but they felt unusual. Still watching, he took another step. Thinking there had been some inner change, the result of his increased weight, perhaps, or of the introduction into his system of some hormonal substance, new to his body but appropriate to his condition, he brought his hands before his eyes, but they seemed quite as usual, his familiar hands. He took some steps around the room. Despite all, he found himself quite able to move quickly and, he thought, with a certain grace. He indulged in one more little leap, which caused the furniture to tremble and the floorboards to shudder, and then sat on the edge of the bed to put on his shoes and socks.

As he went down the hall toward the door to the porch, he saw the old man in the doorway, a small black silhouette with sunlight blazing behind him.

"Good morning," said the doctor, smiling. "Well, here we are. Our first day."

The days of June passed, every day alike, cool mornings and hot blue afternoons. Mice ran on the kitchen floor and squirrels ran on the roof. Spiders caught flies in the window corners in fresh sticky webs. Charles watched the big kitchen spider wrap her fly; he watched until the buzzing stopped. Little brown ants filed across the wall behind the sink, descended to the linoleum, and made for the pantry door. Charles sat in a wooden chair watching them one morning from breakfast to lunch. He put a cornflake in their path and watched them part around it. One ant beneath made it wobble; two climbed aboard and waved their feelers. He laughed out loud.

In the afternoons, after their lunch, the old man slept on the porch. Charles wandered about in the heat looking for a place to lie down. He liked lying on his back with his hands folded on the curve of his big stomach. Sometimes he lay looking up at the clouds with flat bottoms and round tops, moving on toward Montauk and out to sea. No birds except an occasional crow or a slow hawk crossed the sky at that hour. Once a bird's shadow came near him and he watched it fearfully, but it passed by without touching him. He breathed a sigh at his good luck.

As night fell and mist rose in the meadow, deer stepped out of the woods and gazed at the house. Charles stalked toward them, trying not to make a sound with his feet. He got close enough to see their little tails and their shining eyes before they turned and slid back into the dim woods. He was filled with tenderness for the creatures and their fawns. He would have liked to see where they lay down to sleep. Sometimes, in the daytime, he found their dark droppings glistening under the trees near the house, and he knew they had ventured nearer in the moonlight when he was sleeping.

Once, at night, he raised his head from sleep and heard thin barks from the woods. A cluster of yaps resolved into a long wail that trailed away on a single tone to near silence, followed by faint whimpering. A creature was suffering.

His heart was torn for it, whatever it was, whatever had happened to it. The world was full of pain. He turned his head from side to side. The moonlight blazed at him through the window.

The doctor planted some zinnias and a small vegetable garden: two tomato plants, two cucumber seeds, two squash seeds, and a short row of lettuce. Charles helped dig and rake.

Although he had imagined he would use the car to shop and to explore the villages and the farms nearby, he did not. The car sat where he had left it. He scythed around it. From time to time he ran the motor.

All their provisions were brought by the doctor on his tricycle. When he saw the tricycle wobbling toward the house, Charles waited to help with the packages. He was always eager to see what they were going to eat. In July, day after day, it was peas. One evening, Charles was sitting beside the old man in the garden while he shelled peas into a bowl with rabbits on it, blue rabbits on a gray bowl. His fingers moving against the pea pods were pale and thin. The air was still and the brushing of his dry fingers against the smooth skin of the pods made an audible whisper punctuated by a steady popping as the peas dropped first into the bowl and then upon the rising green mound. "Go into the pantry," said the doctor, "and get another bowl."

Charles pulled himself up from his chair and crossed the lawn. The house declared to his nostrils that it was empty. Perhaps it was because it had been empty for so long that it so quickly gave up the imprint of their comings and goings and reverted to its private creakings, its own smell, and its own temperature: silent, musty, and cool. There was no other bowl with rabbits in the pantry. He wanted one with rabbits and so he took a long time, standing in the dim kitchen opening cupboard doors, until at length he came upon a small yellow bowl, rabbitless but with a pleasing wiry crackle, and returned to his chair next to the doctor. "I got one," he said. The doctor gave him a share of the peas. He took one and held it between his thumb and forefinger. The skin of the pod was waxy and dusty and fit smoothly over its cargo of seeds. It was cool to the touch and, although dry, felt moist. Turning it over in his hands, he sought a point of entry but there was no obvious access. He twisted the top apart from the bottom, crushing the pod and letting some of the peas fall into the grass. Of the ones that remained, he ate one and dropped the others into the bowl. Taking another pod, he made an incision along the seam with his thumbnail. The two halves opened easily and the peas fell into the bowl. Then he set the bowl down on the grass and looked across the lawn to where darkness was beginning to thicken under the maple trees.

"Did this ever happen to anyone before?"

"The Romans shelled peas. That is well known."

"No, no."

"No, I was joking. I knew what you were asking."

"*Athena emerged full-blown from her father's head*. It said that in my book at school."

"That's one, then," said the doctor.

"That doesn't count," said Charles.

"I agree," said the old man. "It doesn't."

There was a long silence.

"Why me?" asked Charles. He smelled his finger where the flesh of the pea pod had lodged under his nail. The smell made him think of green watery places.

"*Why me? Why me?* you ask." Now the doctor too put down the pea pods and his bowl. He looked toward the long shadows and the darkening trees. Then he turned to Charles. "Once upon a time," he said, "there was a man who had two little daughters. He lived in a beautiful country where the fields came right up to the towns, and in the forests grew only trees, no bushes. In his garden there were raspberries and currants, and there his daughters played with their dolls and dried their hair in the sunshine."

Charles closed his eyes to listen to the story. He could see the little girls playing in the garden and the red raspberries growing against the house.

"Was the man you?" he asked.

"When the day came that they had to get out of the house, out of the garden, the little girls took the bird in the birdcage and each one took a doll, and the wife took a quilt and pillows so they would have something to sleep on, and the man took some books, and they walked on the road close together, ducking down from time to time when there was danger, sometimes hiding in the ditches, sometimes running, sometimes crossing fields to try to hide in the woods."

"Yes?" said Charles. "Then?"

"The story has a bad end," said the old man.

"But it was long ago," said Charles.

"It was."

"Is it why you are helping me?"

"In part," said the old man.

"What is the other part?"

"You know. I told you. So I could be here once more."

From one day to another the old man looked different. On some days he unfolded himself from the sofa and tottered to the sunshine, stopping to rest two or three times before he reached the porch. Charles, following so he wouldn't fall, saw him holding the doorframe for support, looking toward the blazing sunshine, transparent like a fish in a tank or, since he seemed to grow drier every day, like an insect shriveling in its case. And on those days Charles feared for him, and for himself. At other times, he seemed sturdy, a sturdy old man.

In August, there were weeks of intense heat broken at last by three days of heavy rain. The rain and the wind shook the house, shutters slammed, windowpanes trembled in their loose frames. Outside, the trees bent and waved by day and by night. Then the storm subsided, the sky cleared, and the air grew cold. The doctor and Charles made a fire of applewood in the fireplace and ate their supper in front of it. For supper, they had the first tomato from the garden, sliced, with mayonnaise. With it they ate peanut butter sandwiches; because of the storm, the doctor hadn't been able to get to the village. The tomato could have used another day on the vine, they agreed. It should have had one more day of sunshine. The tomatoes to come would be even more delicious. A pleasure worth waiting for, the doctor said.

Charles went to bed, leaving the old man by the fire, but he was awakened by voices, and after a while, when they persisted, he got out of bed and returned to the living room, where he discovered, to his astonishment, confusion, and quite unexpected pleasure, Gloria, wearing a hat with a bow, sitting in his chair, facing the doctor, with her square black pocketbook on her lap under her folded hands.

"Gloria!" he shouted. The firelight glowed on the curves of her heart-shaped face. She smiled at the extravagance of his greeting but accepted, rather shyly, his embrace. "Mr. Hamilton," she said, "like I was telling the doctor, I come out to see how you two was getting on." She had brought his mail in two shopping bags, as well as a few tidbits to eat. She knew, she said, that they had been living on men's cooking and had no doubt but that a little fried chicken and some muffins would not be unwelcome. The shopping bags were on the floor. Her daughter, she explained, had driven her out here. And they had wandered for hours before they nosed up the right dirt road. But her daughter and granddaughter, who were in the car, waiting, asleep probably, would not come in. She just wanted to see with her own two eyes that they were all right, the doctor and Charles.

Charles edged away from the firelight, not wanting to be inspected too closely. He pushed the sofa to a spot between the two chairs, but away from the fire, and lay down. The two talked, and he listened. They spoke of people they had known in their building, people who had lived there years ago: children who had grown up and gone away, old people who had died. They reminded each other of Gloria's mother and of her husband. The rising and falling of their voices and the flickering of the fire made Charles have to close his eyes. He slept for a moment and then woke up. Then he slept again. Once he heard, or thought he heard, Gloria say, "And those blessed little girls," and he opened his eyes at once, but it seemed he was wrong; the conversation had taken no such turn. At last he gave up trying to follow what they were saying and closed his eyes, letting the murmur of their voices come and go.

He slept.

When he woke, it was morning. The room smelled of wood ashes. The air was cool and fresh. He got up and put the two bags of mail in his closet.

One morning, at breakfast, they heard the squeal of brakes. The doctor raised his head. As he did every day, he had broken his roll into small pieces, which he ate one after another between sips of tea. This morning, however, he only ate one piece, with his chin pointed up and his head tilted to one side. Charles tried to listen for whatever the doctor was listening for, but he heard nothing. The doctor stood up. It was not one of his good mornings. Unsteadily, he went to the door. The breeze stirred his hair. "I heard something," he said over his shoulder.

The night had been cold. The garden was still misty. Charles followed the old man, afraid he would fall as he made his way down the sandy path.

"Something," he said again.

The grass was soaking and cold. The doctor walked fast and Charles walked beside him. Birds were singing loudly and the morning light glistened on the leaves.

When they reached the paved road, at first they saw nothing, although they looked to the right and to the left, but Charles, looking back to his right into the glare of the sunlight, saw what appeared to be a shadow on the road.

The old man looked where he was looking.

"It's nothing," said Charles. "A shadow."

But it was not nothing, he saw. And the old man, despite his worsening vision, also seemed to see that it was not nothing. A large animal was lying in the road. The doctor began to run toward the creature and Charles ran with him. The animal was moving its legs and its head was raised to look toward them as they drew near. It was attempting to draw itself to its feet to escape them, a doe the color of bread, which had been struck by the automobile whose brakes they had heard screech from the house. Little fingers of her blood trickled away from where she was lying on the crown of the road toward the edge of the pavement. From the distance these fingers were silvery, but when Charles and the doctor were within a few feet the silver changed to red. It was flowing from beneath her. Her hoofs made a clacking sound on the macadam, a spasmodic tattoo. She looked from one to the other. Her body arched and rose into the air as though a spring had been released, throwing her up, and then as though the same spring had recoiled she was thrown down to the roadway, landing so that her other side, her injured side, was uppermost. Now they saw her wound, through which white bones and glistening red showed how mortally she was hurt. The doctor took a step closer to her. Then he stopped and waited. Her dark eye looked up. With terror she moved her head from side to side. The doctor sat down beside her on the highway and extended his legs so that when she could no longer hold up her head it would fall upon his thigh. Her legs were still but for a quiver. Her little tail shuddered.

"There, darling," said the old man.

Charles leaned down, pained and helpless. "Can anything be done?" he asked. Her pelt was twitching, her notched ears trembled. The doctor drew his hands along her ears.

"Yes," he said. "Stand up and watch that something doesn't come along to run us all over."

Charles straightened up.

The morning breeze was still and the sun warm on his cheeks. At first, as he stood guard looking down the road, the silence seemed absolute, but after a few minutes he heard the *pop-pop* of a tennis game from beyond the woods and the laugh of a man's voice and the cry of a woman's. He heard a plane in the sky and automobiles on the highway far away.

Looking down at the animal, he saw how the little flange of fur on the rear of her flanks crested and how the hair changed from brown to white, from public to intimate. Would it be possible, he wondered, to bring her back to the house and sew up the parts of her insides that were torn and close up her wound with neat stitches and care for her?

The doctor looked up at him.

"Damn you, eyes, look your fill," he said.

Charles let himself look his fill. When he raised his eyes, he saw a fawn, the poor creature's, no doubt, standing uncertainly before them in the shade where the pin oaks shadowed the road. The animal sidestepped toward them, its small hoofs like high heels on a little girl and its tail going round and round in circles like a toy. The doe must hear it, Charles thought, or smell it, for he saw her lift her head.

The doctor clapped his hands. "Scat," he shouted. The fawn took two little clicking steps and leaped into the woods. The sound of leaves brushed and twigs breaking lasted only a minute.

The deer shook all over and died.

"Dead," said the doctor. He stood up slowly with great difficulty, pushing himself up with his forearms and then his hands.

"All right. Come. Let's throw her in the ditch," he said.

"In the ditch?" said Charles. "Shouldn't we bury her?"

"In the ditch," said the old man, wiping his hands on his sweater.

"No," said Charles. "Let's. Please, let's."

The doctor said he was too old and too weak. A dead body is heavy, he said, far too heavy to drag all the way back to the house.

"I want to," said Charles.

"You shouldn't either, in your condition," said the doctor with a little cackle.

"I'll get the car," said Charles. He proposed they lift her into the trunk and bury her in the garden.

The doctor suggested that Charles consider the fact that animals who die in the woods don't have funerals.

Charles answered that she had not died in the woods. He walked back to the house to get his car. As he was nosing down the dirt road, the doctor appeared. Charles stopped.

The old man stuck his head in the window. "Why do you want me to exhaust myself? Don't you want me to last until it's time for me to unburden you?"

"I'll do it by myself, then," said Charles.

He turned onto the paved road. When he was alongside the animal, he drove onto the shoulder of the road and stopped. He opened the door and carefully eased himself past the steering wheel. As he was getting out, he saw he was about to step into her blood. Quickly he drew back his foot. Grasping the doorframe with both hands, he stuck his feet out past the blood and pushed himself clear.

She looked smaller now. Her neck was long, she seemed to be more neck than anything else. She was flat, sunken. Charles stood in his white shirt, looking down at her. He saw tears below her eyes. He bent to look more closely. They seemed to be tears, dark and wet. He extended his hand to feel if they were really wet, but withdrew it. Charged with the job of burying her, he was stymied by the blood, by her torn side, and by what threatened to spill from the wound should he lift her, assuming that he could lift her. He wanted to lift her in his arms and carry her back to the garden, where he would bury her in a spacious grave. He imagined her weight in his arms. Her head would rest on his shoulder, he would grasp her long neck, and her loose legs would dangle and bump against him.

It wasn't finished until dark; it had taken the whole day. Charles was trembling with fatigue. Of course, he had not been able to carry her, smeared and bloody as she was. He had struggled to drag her close to the car and left her lying on the bank where her blood percolated into the sand while he walked back to the house to get a length of rope. Because there was to be no lifting her up. The poor animal would pollute the trunk of the car, very likely forever; it wasn't any longer a question of mere blood.

Perspiring in the sunshine, he tied her forelegs together and then her rear legs and fastened them to the rear bumper. Twice cars slowed as they passed. One stopped alongside and a young woman said, "A dog? You killed a dog?" She looked more closely and made a grimace, her mouth square with disgust. In the back seat of her car a German shepherd growled. He showed his teeth and tried to push his head out the front window. She drove away. Charles wiped the sweat from his eyes with the back of his forearm. His shirt clung to him. Having tested the knots he started the car and drove very slowly, staying on the shoulder, thinking her fur would be less harmed by bumping over the weeds and grass clumps than by scraping along the road. He drove with the door open, steering with his right hand, leaning out so he could look back. When he reached the dirt road he made a wide arc and got out to straighten the ropes. He saw she was already much damaged. With his feet he pushed the body so it was directly behind the car and then drove slowly down the dirt road. Here the hump between the ruts and the grass, which had grown tall, made her twitch and jump as she was pulled along.

When he reached the end of the sand road, he drove over the tall grass. He stopped where he planned to bury her, at the edge of the woods. There he tried to loosen the ropes, but they had been pulled into knots too tight to untie. On his way to the kitchen for a knife, he saw the doctor on the porch. He didn't look up. The kitchen was still cool. Charles drank a glass of water and set the glass down in the sink, but he picked it up again and filled it once more. He drank the second glass before he opened the loose drawer and chose a knife. This time the old man nodded as he went by. In his hand he was holding a palmetto fan, which he slowly passed back and forth in front of his face. The leaves were still. There was no breeze at all.

When Charles reached the body, he saw it was covered with flies crawling thickly on it and flying in the air above. He tried to interfere with the circling layers by pushing his arm abruptly into their midst, thinking they would disperse. Their heavy little bodies bumped his forearm. He shuddered, there were so many of them. They were being drawn from the woods, there was no beating them back. He hurried to saw through the rope, but the knife was blunt. At last, however, her forelegs and then her hind legs fell to the ground. He felt relieved to see her freed. Tearing a branch from the nearest oak, he shook the leafy ends fiercely over her body to give himself a moment in which to cover her with leaves and grass so she could lie undisturbed while he drove the car away. The smell of the car bothered him, the smell of hot metal and gasoline. The car bothered him, winking in the sunlight.

When he had parked the car in its usual spot, he went into the shed and stood there blinking in the dark, waiting until he could see the spade hanging on the back wall where its handle fit over a triangle of nails. He reached up and brought down the spade. Now things are getting done, he thought, as he returned over the tall grass with the spade on his shoulder, but when he set the tip of the blade on the ground and tried to force it through the surface, webbed with roots and bound soil, he understood the size of his task.

It was not until late in the afternoon that he succeeded, with the help of a shovel and a pickax, in removing turf from a large enough area to begin to dig deep. He mounded the dark topsoil all around the edges of the rectangle. The disturbed earthworms slid out of sight. Perspiring heavily and resting more often and for longer intervals, he urged himself on.

The house was in shadow, and the entire meadow as well, by the time the hole was deep and square enough for him to set down the spade. He tugged the animal over the grass and then, so as not to throw her into the grave, he stepped down into the hole and pulled her toward him. Lifting her in his arms, he laid her on the ground at his feet. Now that he had got her in the grave, lying on her side, with her wound beneath her, she no longer looked ragged and disheveled. He arranged her limbs, straightening them as best he could. She seemed to be standing still, with her neck extended and her head pointed upward slightly as though smelling the air. She looked lovely, alert and vulnerable. He squatted. Maintaining his balance with one hand, with the other he smoothed the fur on her neck and flanks so that all the hairs lay smooth. At once, the fading light turned her silver. He lifted the spade to begin to cover her with earth when an idea struck him and he set the spade down. Bending with difficulty, he reached to change the position of her legs, moving the front two forward and the back ones out so she seemed to be running. Running away, out of danger. Satisfied, he stood up and grasped the spade.

When the displaced earth had been returned to the hole, Charles reversed the spade and with its back smoothed the soil. Out of the corner of his eye he saw the doctor step sidewise off the porch, holding the banister for support, and start toward him, walking unsteadily across the meadow. As the old man drew near, Charles walked around the grave, beating down the earth with the back of the shovel, creating a flowerlike form of concentric circles made by the repeated impression of the back of the shovel, each one like a petal. He was finished. She was buried; he had made a nice grave.

The old man stood beside him. "Done?" he asked.

"Yes," said Charles. "Done."

The old man made an abrupt movement with one hand to steady himself. He caught Charles by the forearm and held on to regain his balance. The two men stood together beside the grave. The air smelled of fresh earth. Rustling and tapping sounded from the woods. The light was nearly gone. Now that the job was done, Charles was overtaken with fatigue. The porch seemed far away. He considered sitting down in the grass just where he was, but instead walked back with the old man on his arm, taking small steps over the uneven meadow in the darkness. He was worn out.

On the porch he sat in the rocking chair and closed his eyes. The doctor went inside to bring something cool to drink.

"Iced tea," Charles requested.

"No, hot is better," he said, letting the screen door slam. Charles rested. As darkness fell, the air cooled quickly. The smell of grasses reached him, and at the edge of the woods he imagined he saw the fawn's eyes shine. He shifted in the rocking chair, which creaked. The boards of the porch floor creaked. A breeze blew the shaggy gray curtain out the unscreened window, where it bellied, then fell against the shingled side of the porch. It made a scratchy sound. The musty smell of the old house came out to the porch through the open windows. Inside, the doctor was clattering things. The deer was lying in her grave. What had happened to her was terrible, but she had been comforted. She had started her life in the grave. In that,

64

there was justice. What would happen now, would happen.

Charles heard the doctor shuffling in the hall. He hitched the rocking chair toward the door and held it open. The old man was carrying two glasses of tea on a tray. Charles held the tray while the old man sat down.

"Sugar?" said the doctor, handing him the box of sugar cubes.

Charles did as the old man did. He drank the tea with a cube of sugar in his teeth. The sweet hot tea made his eyes water.

"What will happen now?" he asked. "What do you think will happen now?"

"Well," said the old man, "one thing that will happen is that we will all lie in the earth."

"Yes," said Charles. "I know that. But I mean what do you think will happen to me now?"

It was fully dark. Black trees, black meadow under the sky; no moon, a few stars.

"Ah!" cried the doctor. "A shooting star." He stood up and leaned over the railing to look up. "You saw?"

Charles had not seen. He watched the sky.

"Another, another! You saw?"

"No," said Charles. "Where, where?"

Clumsily they bumped the chairs down the two steps of the porch and dragged them away from the house. They sat in the dark looking up.

"What will happen? Ordinary life will close back around you like water when you throw a stone in. Assuming all goes well, that is. And then in one or two years you will have drawn a curtain of oblivion over his beginnings. You know, in Europe, in Poland, when I used to be called for the accouchement, the screams would be heard up and down the whole street. And in the summer, when the windows were opened, in the houses you would hear. Children would cover their ears. Screams that would cut your heart. There are few pains that equal those pains of women. And yet afterward she forgets. They speak of the

pain, the women together, for their whole lives, but they
don't remember it. And so you will not be unlike them,
you will not remember that he came into the world in an
unusual way. If you see what I mean."

"Ah," said Charles, "I saw one."

The doctor continued. "You will be one of those papa's—daddy's, I should say—with a little child. With the
mother dead, or in the sanitarium, as it used to be, or run
off with some Hungarian to Paris, or as they do now living
in Vermont with another lady, or even as your Amanda,
gone to be a lawyer to take care of the lakes and trees. You
will forget this peculiar shape you have taken and the way
we lived together in this old house. You will barely remember me."

"You lived in Poland? I thought you lived in Germany
before you came here to the U.S.," said Charles. "Were
you—are you, I mean—Jewish?"

"My poor boy," said the doctor.

"Sorry," said Charles.

"No, no," said the old man.

There was a long silence. Charles felt cross that the old
man had called him "poor boy." But at the same time he
was filled with a delicious feeling. He thought of the
expression "unearthly happiness" and he would have liked
to say it aloud, but fearing to appear foolish, he did not.
Compromising, he said the single word "happiness" out
loud. If childishness was its price, then he was childish.
The old man had grumpily left him alone and he had buried
the deer all by himself. He knew his happiness was partially
derived from having struggled for her the whole day long.
Now he was resting in the cool while one after another
meteors glided down and disappeared. His happiness had
earthly connections as well. Under his bare feet, he felt
the grass, the stubble scratchy and the fresh blades cool,
and beneath the grass the still-warm earth.

"Of course I knew you were Jewish," he said. "I thought
you probably were. I just didn't like to ask."

"Well, why not?" asked the doctor. "You thought it a disgrace?"

Charles did not know what to answer the old man, but it seemed not to matter, for while he was trying to think what to say, the doctor reached over and took his hand. "You have been a good patient," he said. "A good patient and a good companion. Now go inside and go to sleep."

"Shouldn't I eat something?" said Charles, standing up.

"Later I'll bring you some soup. I have to do some things."

Charles lay awake, alert for sounds, for changes in the air, for lights in the sky. He smelled steam and heard sounds of metal from the kitchen. Then he closed his eyes. He continued to hear the doctor moving about, shuffling, opening and closing drawers. He heard water running. He slept for a short time and woke again. The doctor was still moving about. When he could distinguish the objects in his room and color was appearing in the sky, he heard the old man's footsteps coming down the hall. He entered the room.

"It is my feeling," he said, "that we should go ahead with it now. We must not wait too long."

The child was delivered, a boy. It was healthy. It was given no name at first. Charles lay in bed for a day or two but quickly regained his strength.

He was never able to remember the weeks that followed. It is true that he never tried very hard. Sometimes, in the years to come, something—a smell, perhaps, or a slant of sunlight with the motes running in it a certain way, or a particular draft of air passing his cheek as a door opened or shut—might make him stop what he was doing and stand still, with his nose in the air like a dog, taut with the sense that only the thinnest film hung between him and recollection. At such moments, he hovered, or so he thought, near the possibility of taking action and with a forceful thrust pushing away whatever were the cobwebs that hid the memory of those events, those feelings. But whether or not he could have, for one reason or another he never did try.

One memory remained: he was lying on his side on the bed with his head propped on his hand. The infant was sleeping near his chest. The memory provided him no picture of the baby; he felt it to be there. It was afternoon, the room was full of a greenish light, and Charles, idly casting his eyes about the room, observed that his vision had sharpened to quite a noticeable degree. His eyeglasses were folded on the table. Without them he saw the wall-paper of the far wall: the lake, the two swans, the graceful boy leaning over the maiden. A fly walked up the wall. He saw its feet. Was this an adaptive phenomenon engineered to help the newly delivered beast guard her cub, or pup, against whatever marauders prowled? He checked again. No doubt about it, even his peripheral vision was uncannily sharp. He wondered if it would last.

They cared for the baby together. The doctor was quite competent, had secured the various necessities for feeding, for bathing, had smuggled them in, so to speak, when Charles wasn't looking and had tucked them away until they were needed. He seemed to know exactly how much to warm the water, just how to convert the packets of powder to a milky liquid, which the baby weakly swallowed at first, then sucked greedily until with a film of perspiration upon his tiny brow he slept as though drugged. Charles let him hold his finger while he drank. His hair was fine and black, the soles of his feet were red.

Charles gave no thought to the future. Or rather he seemed to think that things would go on just as they were. Time had slowed. The doctor brought little meals to him. He dozed and looked out of the window. He sat on the porch with the infant beside him. He walked to the maple tree and back.

One morning when the baby was several weeks old,

Charles, walking in the sunshine, checking, as he had been accustomed to do, the zucchini for size and the tomatoes for ripeness, thought with a flash of pleasure of taking the car out for a spin. Passing the doctor, who was sitting on the porch with the baby in his basket beside him, Charles announced what he was about to do and said he would be soon back. The old man, who was stroking the infant's head, looked up at him with pale blue eyes, lighter, Charles thought, than ever, and gave a little nod. A physicianly little nod, thought Charles, as if to say, Just as I expected. He carefully backed the car to the sand road and then nosed out to the blacktop. He passed the spot where the deer had lain. It seemed to have happened months ago, years, in fact. He drove through the village and out to the expressway, where he had not been since the day in June he had driven out with the old man wobbling in the front seat. Now it was late in September. The tall grasses at the side of the road were bleached white. The full dense crowns of the trees were unmarked by any sign that summer had ended, but the sumac and the maple striplings showed here and there a flash of orange or of red. The sun glittered on the hood of the car. The sky was blue. Gradually he increased his speed. He turned up the radio. The noise and the speed and the bright sun demanded a recklessness he was glad to give. He drove all the way to Montauk Point and sat there, with the engine off, and looked at the ocean. It flicked with wind, with waves, with light.

After a while, he started the engine, wheeled around in the parking lot, and drove back.

"I think I'm going to go back," he said to the doctor. "I'm going back."

"Yes," said the old man. "You go back. It's time. But I'll stay."

For the rest of the morning Charles sat beside the telephone, making arrangements, setting things up. Gloria's daughter would meet him at the apartment. Until the agency could send a nursemaid, she would stay. Perhaps she would even do for the long haul. He would have to see.

Again he asked the old man if he was sure he wanted to stay on alone. "Oh, yes," he said and asked if Charles wanted to take anything back to the city as a souvenir. "Oh, no," said Charles, pushing clothes into his bag. He found his good shoes in the back of the closet in his room and rubbed them with a rag. They looked passable, he thought, but his jacket and trousers did not. They would do, though, since he had only to put the car in the garage in the basement of the building, from which he would take the elevator straight up without having to go out on the street. The baby, sleeping in his laundry basket, they secured in the back seat of the car.

"I don't know how to thank you," said Charles. A handshake seemed the wrong farewell.

"Of course you don't," said the old man. "I don't know how to thank you either."

Charles touched the old man's cheek. He had never seemed so small.

"Good-bye," said Charles.

"Good-bye, Charles," he said. "Good-bye, dear baby," he said, leaning over the baby in the back seat. "Have a good trip."

Just before the entrance to the expressway, Charles turned back. There was something he did want: he wanted the bowl with the rabbits. When he got back to the house, he ran up the steps, calling, "Here we are again!" but there was no answer. He looked for the doctor all over the house, but he was not to be seen. Wondering if he had set out for the village, he opened the shed door, but the tricycle sat in its accustomed spot. *I took the bowl with the rabbits,* he wrote on a piece of paper that he set in the middle of the kitchen table, securing it under the sugar bowl. He sur-

mised the old man had gone for a walk. *See you soon,* he
added. He wrapped the bowl with the rabbits in newspaper
and set it on the floor in the back of the car. The baby
stirred and pursed his lips.

Closing the car door quietly so the baby wouldn't wake
up, he gave a last look at the house, the porch and the
open windows, the toolshed, but then, instead of getting
in, he stopped with his hand on the door and stood without
moving for a long time.

"Should I go? Do you think I should go?" he asked at
length, convinced the doctor was standing right next to
him.

He heard himself talking to nobody.

He would have to decide himself, he thought, one way
or the other.

It was late afternoon. The wind was blowing, shaking
the leaves. At a sound from the house, he looked quickly
around, but it was, he saw, only the front door banging.
He would have to close it when he left. If he left, he
corrected himself.

Preoccupied, he didn't hear the baby begin to cry until
the first whimpers had turned to wails and the infant,
drawn up into a ball, had propelled himself to the end of
his basket, where he lay pressed against the wicker, writh-
ing, with his red fists making circles in the air. He was
gasping for breath.

Disconcerted, Charles reached in and fished him out. It
was not clear to him what to do next. These decisions had
always been in the doctor's hands. Holding the baby tightly
against his chest, he bent and felt in the basket for the
precautionary bottle the doctor had prepared. He hurried
to the porch, where he sat down in the doctor's rocking
chair and pushed the nipple at the infant's mouth. He had
to touch the child's lips with the nipple several times before
he stopped crying long enough to suck, but when he was
finally drinking noisily, Charles, himself calmer, looked

down at him attentively, as though for the first time. He observed him for a moment and then he raised his head in surprise.

He hasn't got a name, he thought. I haven't named him. It was a serious omission, he thought. I have to find a name for him. It's the first order of business.

Later, holding him in the crook of his arm, he walked from room to room. "Adam?" he said, starting at the beginning of the alphabet. "Benjamin? A bit heavy. Charles? Douglas? No, I think not." It was a strange thing, he thought, that he didn't know the old man's first name.

He set the baby down on the kitchen counter, propped with towels, as the doctor used to.

"This is an egg," he said.

The baby was watching him.

"And this," he said, gesturing, "is a frying pan."

He broke the egg into the bowl with the rabbits.

"I am going to make myself an omelet," he said. "Then we'll find you a good name. And then we'll see."

When the Pipes Froze

꙰ ꙰ On Friday, January second, we went up to Ashfield for a winter weekend, or so we thought, with new cross-country skis and long underwear, leaving the children at home to write term papers and stay out late with their friends. By the time we turned off the highway, the sun had set. It was bitterly cold. When we arrived at the house, my husband, with a suitcase in one hand and the key in the other, went at once to open the door, saying he would turn up the heat and come back for whatever I couldn't manage. I followed with my arms full, but when I entered the shed I found him hunched over the padlock at the side door of the house, with his gloves thrown down on the floor, in the fading light. "Christ," he said, not looking up, "the power is off."

"The bulb," I said, "couldn't it just be the bulb?" Setting down my bags, I felt overhead for the string to the shed light.

"I tried it," said Richard. "I think we're in trouble."

I watched him struggling with bare hands over the stiff lock. I knew he was fearing for the pipes, new pipes, all of them, which we had had installed, along with the new heating system, the new wiring, the new kitchen equipment, when we redid the house as soon as we bought it two years ago. The warmth I had brought with me from the car was escaping, and I stamped my feet on the uneven shed floor.

"Don't do that," said Richard. "You're making everything shake."

At last he pushed open the door. In the dark winter light

the house was cold and quiet. The furnace, the pump, and the refrigerator all were silent. We walked from room to room, without speaking, to find the damage. There was no sound but our own footsteps. At first there was nothing to see. The house was neat and simple and didn't look as though anything had happened to it at all. While Richard took a flashlight down to the cellar, I opened the bathroom door. Forgetting the temperature, I expected to see water leaking from the walls and spreading on the floor. There was nothing on the floor, but upon looking closely I noticed a fine crack in the toilet tank, which held, as I saw when I lifted the lid, a neat rectangle of ice. Carefully I put back the lid and wondered what Richard was finding below. I shuddered with cold and clapped my hands in their mittens.

In the kitchen, on the table near the window, a brown bowl we had been given as a housewarming present was filled with ice. I must have thrown the chrysanthemums away when we were cleaning up the last time we were here but left the water, which had frozen, and in freezing had cracked the bowl, letting a little water seep through the crack and spread on the table where, in its turn, it froze.

Richard called me to come down to the cellar.

"It's bad," he said, aiming the flashlight so I could see the pump. The pump head was split. He showed me the line of the break along the side and straight across the top. We were both shaking with cold. As we leaned over the pump, the beam of light lit our smoking breaths. Richard pointed the flashlight at the holding tank and I saw it was frozen solid. It was all bad, very bad. He was certain pipes were broken all over the house.

Upstairs I showed him a bottle of tonic I had found in the kitchen cupboard, with its sides splintered and a plug of frozen tonic coming out of its neck.

"Put it down," he said. "You'll cut yourself. That's all we need." He waved it away and sat down at the kitchen table with his head in his hands. "I knew I should have come up to drain the pipes," he said. Last winter, the men who repaired the house advised us to keep the furnace on; it would be better for the new wood, they said, and for the plaster as well. They would keep an eye on the house for us, they said. This year autumn weather had lasted until just before Christmas. We had trusted the furnace and the thermostat to keep going until we got here.

Suddenly Richard picked up the broken bowl in both hands, raised it above his head, and hurled it at the wall. Pieces of pottery skidded on the floor. The chunk of ice rolled as far as the fireplace and stopped. "Sorry," he said, as he got up to get the broom. "I just had to." Then we both laughed a little and I patted him on the arm. I wished we could just drive away and leave it all behind.

Richard called the power company, the neighbors, the electrician, and the plumber. The plumber's wife said he was out working on pipes. We should keep on trying to call him, she said. The neighbors had not lost their power but they were sympathetic, they knew what trouble we were in. The power company's phone was busy.

It was too cold to stay in the house any longer. Holding the flashlight in one hand, I dialed Howard Johnson's and reserved a room for the night. "But let's not eat there," I said. Richard agreed we didn't have to eat there. We would eat at Herm's instead. As we drove down the winding road with moonlit fields and black barns on either side, I felt a guilty relief. We could do nothing about what had happened now. It was something for the electrician, for the power company, for Mr. Daisy, the plumber.

Herm's was warm and brightly lit. The tablecloths were red and the napkins were green. We ordered whiskey sours, and I stood up at once to go to the salad bar. I put cherry tomatoes on my plate, corn relish, three-bean salad, pickled beets, pimentos, and shredded carrot salad. I drank my whiskey sour, and when we had finished our drinks we ordered two more. For dinner we had scrod with Newburg sauce and for dessert I had pumpkin pie. While we ate we talked about the children, about Richard's department and some promotions due to be considered soon. We said nothing about the pipes, but as we left the restaurant and the bitter air struck my face, I said, "That all was delicious."

The wind was blowing little swirls of snow around the parking lot. The moon had set, and the sky was black, clear, and full of stars. Richard started the car.

"Everything we ate was orange," he said. It had all come back to him. He was struck with the enormity of it: not the cost, which would of course be great, not the trouble, the inconvenience, the ruin of our weekend, but something more deeply distressing, something that evoked shame in him, and misery. I saw he felt that the cold, knowing he was not a worthy person, had wrapped itself around his house and taken its rightful toll in cracked, twisted, and burst materials. He could hardly talk for the weight of it.

The house had looked innocent as we drove into the yard, and unharmed. It gave no sign that anything had happened. A light snow lay on the ground, old snow, thinly glazed with ice. Black, hollow stalks of sweet cicely and the brittle stems of the rosebushes, pushed back and forth by the wind, scratched against the siding. The house, with its shingled roof, front door, four windows, everything plain and symmetrical, looked quite as usual. But the cold had pressed against it. At first, the cold had merely run around the outside, testing for an opening here, a loose pane there, seeking entrance through the ways we go in and out, like a child, or a dog trying to slip in between his master's legs. Later, it sought cracks, like a mouse or a bug. Finally, as the temperature fell to below freezing, and continued to fall, the cold, on which particular day we did not know, Christmas Day, perhaps, or the day after, had hugged the house to it. For by then, the cold had sunk through the air into the earth, reaching under the house with icy fingers that met in the hard subsoil beneath and moved up to grip the house from below. When had the power gone off? When had the water in the bowl begun to freeze? The kitchen clock was stopped at eleven twenty-five. At eleven twenty-five one night, the power had gone off and with it the oil burner, and gradually the house had lost its heat and the pipes had frozen.

That this had happened in our absence, invisibly, made me think about the mystery of the great powers which exact events without our participation: the rising sun, the moon dragging behind her the tides, winter creeping down from the north, the seas spilling over the land, beaches emerging, waves of weather streaming overhead. I thought of the first days of the child in the womb and the tumor beginning to creep beyond its confines. While we were celebrating Christmas Eve or eating Christmas dinner, our house, white in the dark night, catching whatever light there was, starlight or cloudy moonlight, began to freeze and, helpless, suffered injuries whose extent we could not yet determine. Whatever was to break was broken and lay cracked and split. The damage was hidden, but when the heat came on again and the ice melted, water would seep from the pipes into the plaster walls. I entertained the hope that despite the laws of physics and country lore perhaps in our case some dispensation would have been made and either these pressures would not have been exerted or some other avenue would have been made to spare our plumbing. I did not express this thought to my husband, knowing it for a wanton thought, unworthy even as a hope, betraying me for a child.

To enter our wing of the motel, we had to open a glass door, which bore a sign reading YOUR ROOM KEY OPENS THIS DOOR. Inside, we inhaled the hot, circulated air of the hall. Richard opened the door of our room, and I felt for the light switch, which responded to my finger, but in an unsatisfying way. The lights went on, but the switch made no click; it merely retreated slightly into its holder.

Quickly, I observed the two double beds, the beige bed-spreads, the carpet, mirrors, lamps, the soundproofing panel in the ceiling, the closed door to the bathroom, the television.

"What a nice room," I said.

Richard had gone straight to the telephone and was dialing the plumber.

In the house there had been a cold, dry smell, sad, vulnerable, and enduring. It was the smell of life withdrawn, life retreating into itself, not absent but dormant and cold, the smell of cold wood. The motel room smelled invulnerable. Whatever substances had been used in the construction of its surfaces gave off a smell that was hard to breathe. Had it not been so cold out, I would have pushed open the plaid curtains with the plastic lining and opened a window. Even though we had just eaten, I picked up the menu for the restaurant. I turned on the television. I wanted to enjoy the motel, use all the plastic glasses, shine my shoes with the cloth that was just for shining shoes, bathe in the bathtub whose subsequent cleanliness was no concern of mine, dry myself under the orange rays of the ultraviolet fixture in the ceiling. Tomorrow, I thought, I will pocket the unopened little bars of soap.

"The power company says they'll try to get someone there on Monday," Richard said. "The girl said they have more to do than they can handle." He looked better now that he was working on the problem, getting people on the phone, starting on the solution. I wished we could just drive away in the morning and let the pipes freeze, the cellar flood, the branches fall where they would. How could we hold winter at bay?

Once, twenty-five years ago, on the beach at Race Point, near Provincetown, we had set up a pup tent and settled in for the night. We had spread out a plastic bag whose original purpose was to shield the wearer from a gas attack, or so the man in the army-navy store had said, but for us, advised by the helpful salesman, it was a way of protecting our sleeping bag from the damp chill of the sand at night. The tent, being absolutely primitive, had no floor. It was easy to set up, but nonetheless it took us a long time. Holding a tent pole in both hands, I twisted it slowly into the sand, bearing down with all my weight. Richard got his done first and came around to help me. Then we bent down to insert at a neat angle into the sand the metal prongs, unpleasantly scabbed with rust, around which we wrapped the stiff waxy loops of the tent canvas. Although the sun had set, it was still light; evening, but not yet night. The sky was clear, a green sky over a pale ocean. The tent faced the ocean and the east, where darkness would rise; behind us, over the dune, the pinks and yellows of the fading sunset flooded the sky. We had left our car, a Model A we had bought from a man in Brooklyn, at the parking lot and had struggled down to the beach with our equipment for the night. I imagine we had eaten supper. I don't remember carrying food, I don't remember eating, although we had probably brought along chocolate bars, or peaches, just for the fun of eating something in the tent. When everything was ready and our sleeping bag smoothed over the plastic bag, the door flaps fastened and a square of mosquito netting swagged over the door, we knelt on the sand and crawled in to consecrate our little house.

Night fell. The sand cooled. I lay on my stomach with my chin resting on the back of my hand. With the other hand I was gently lifting sand that was still warm from the heat of the day and letting it trickle through my fingers. Richard lay next to me and we looked out the door of the tent toward the ocean. For a long time we lay talking, with our heads near the opening, hearing the rush and fall of the waves, feeling that our lives lay coiled within us, invisible but unique and worthy of our expectations. What were we talking about for so long? We used to talk in those days about the future and the things we wanted to do, where we would travel, how we wanted to live. We also talked about the past, about our parents and our childhoods. We took a great interest in each other's childhoods, which were, in truth, not that long ago ended. We told one another the litany of familial injustices and those wrongs done to us by teachers and other grown-ups. We could talk for hours, for the whole night, and sometimes did, analyzing our short pasts or projecting our long future. We both had psychoanalyses and talked about them to one another, narrating our dreams when we woke up and at night reporting what our analysts had said. We had great expectations. At some time in the future, we would be "cured." Our proper lives would then commence. At that time I would write and have children and we would have exquisite, astonishing sex.

As we murmured and drowsed in our tent, far out at sea we could see heat lightning pulsing on the horizon. It was too far away to hear any thunder. The cold air on our cheeks made the heat of the tent delicious. We slept. When I awoke, it was still dark. The lightning was a lot closer, and I could hear long, slow rumbles of thunder. A bolt of lightning lit the ocean, and I saw the waves breaking on the beach. All at once a wind replaced the breeze and the tent flapped heavily like a sail. My thought that we would soon enjoy the sound of rain overhead was swept away as I realized the storm was upon us. Fat drops spattered the canvas, which shook in the noisy wind. Bolts of lightning followed one upon the other and thunder banged without a pause. As each bolt struck the sand, the beach flared into sight and the air was filled with the smell of hot metal. We crawled out of the tent, which was slapping and twisting in the wind.

"Get away from it," Richard shouted. "It will draw the lightning. Run!"

I ran, but as I ran my feet sank. My legs dragged, and I could not pull my feet out of the soft sand. The rain hit my face in drops so large they hurt. Almost at once my

long hair was soaked and my blue jeans and shirt were wet
and heavy. I fell, got up, and stumbled again, running
unevenly, squinting to see through the rain. Suddenly, I
was struck with fear lest the flashlight I was holding attract
lightning. Without stopping, I threw it as far away as I
could. Panicky, I saw myself as a tiny creature running
from the lightning as it tried to reach around me from
above and strike me through the ring on my finger or the
metal bits at the corners of my pants pockets. Nor did I
know where Richard was in all that noise and darkness
until a bolt that turned the whole beach pink and left a
smell of burned matches showed him stopped ahead, looking back for me and urging me on.

"Come on!" he was shouting. "Come on! Run!"

And I ran.

The next flash of lightning showed the break in the dune
where a white path led to the place we had left the car. As
I staggered over the crest, the sharp beach grass stung my
wet face. Crouching in the trough between the dunes, we
ran on, knowing we were almost safe.

In the car, we gasped for breath, we kissed one another's
wet faces, we put our wet arms around one another. We
were panting and laughing. Our hearts were still thumping
in our chests. Water ran from our hair and clothing down
the channels of the upholstery and made puddles on the
floor. Secure from the lightning by virtue of the thin hard
rubber tires, which, as Richard explained to me, should
the car be struck, would let the lightning go straight down
to the ground, we laughed out loud. We were all right. It
was an adventure, that was all. When we had caught our
breath, we reviewed the whole story, how we had been
lying with that light flickering far away, and suddenly we
were in the middle of the storm, in danger, and the lightning was everywhere, we could hardly run. *Bang, bang,* it
was all around us. There wasn't even a second between
the thunder and the lightning, it was that close. The safety
of the car was as delightful as the warmth and coziness of

the tent had been earlier, but soon enough our excitement waned. Richard started the car and drove slowly through the rain, which flooded the windshield so that the wipers were scarcely able to sweep a fan-shaped clearing before the water ran around them and spilled over again.

We drove into Provincetown and banged on our friend Mary Stebbins's door to tell her about the lightning and the wind. She let us in, but she was half asleep. She had some dry crullers and we ate them and drank some milk to wash them down. I don't remember where we lay down to sleep, but it may have been on her floor.

My friends and I firmly believed in love and we believed in work. We believed that love and work were shields against failure. By failure, we meant the gradual replacement of vitality with the dismal acquisition of things: money, position, or reputation. It seemed that the adults we knew, our parents and our teachers, had all failed in life. Some had simply pursued false goals from the first; others had been deflected from their youthful ideals by one contingency or another. We detected the signs of this failure in the way they dressed and where they lived, in the cars they drove and the garages they parked them in, in the rugs they put on their floors and the pictures on their walls. We saw it as well as in the lectures they gave and in the books they wrote. Richard's friend Stavros showed him a monograph he had found in the stacks written by Walter Stearns, one of their professors, forty years before. It had been his doctoral dissertation. "Do you see," Stavros said, raising his eyebrows and shaking his head, "do you see how *clean* it is? And look what happened to him." Such a thing would never happen to us. How not? One way was by our psychoanalyses.

It was not Richard and I alone who went to psychoanalysts. Most of our friends had psychoanalyses as well. Barbara went to Dr. Thaler on 96th Street and Marilyn went to Dr. Riskin and later to Dr. Bauer, whom she referred to as Inge Riskin and Grete Bauer. Her father was a psychoanalyst and thought she should see a woman. Richard went to Dr. Freeman on Park Avenue and I went to see Dr. Henschel on 92nd Street. Richard's sister, Anne, while she was living in New York, waiting for her husband to come back from Korea, went to Dr. Moskowitz, and Sandra, his younger sister, went to Dr. Reuben. Richard's friend Frank went to the clinic at Bellevue, and Michael went to the Psychiatric Institute at Columbia, which we called "PI." I went to Dr. Henschel three times a week and paid her fifteen dollars a session at first; then, later, twenty dollars. Richard went to Dr. Freeman three times a week also, but he had to pay only ten dollars a week at first until it was raised to twelve-fifty. Aaron and his girlfriend, Lisa, had been interviewed at the New York Psychoanalytic Institute in hopes of being accepted at its clinic, where the fee was a dollar a session, but they both were rejected. We reported to one another how our analysts conducted our sessions: who let you smoke, what happened if you didn't come, did you have to pay even if you canceled, who lay on the couch and who did not. Richard told the story of how Dr. Freeman once fell asleep, and I used to tell about how I didn't say anything for a whole session and Dr. Henschel said nothing either, just went right on knitting. "Knitting?" said my listeners. "She knits? Oh, I couldn't stand that." Dr. Tartak told Susan Gould she should not see a certain boy she was going out with, and a friend of Richard's friend Marvin had been instructed to "refrain from sexual intercourse." Whether that proscription was intended to apply to a short period or to the course of treatment we did not know. Courses of treatment were long. I went to Dr. Henschel from the time I was nineteen until Richard got his Ph.D. and we went to Dijon on a Fulbright for a year. Richard went to Dr. Freeman for nearly as long.

Another way by which we planned never to fail was going to be our "work." We used the word "work" in a special way. "No, we are working," we might say to a friend who telephoned to ask if we wanted to go to the movies. Work to us meant studying philosophy or writing stories. But in fact I hardly wrote anything. From time to time I took out a notebook and made an entry. I described Schrafft's, where Richard worked behind the counter at night. "The woman stirred her coffee without looking down. Her hair was greasy and her fingernails afflicted with dark red polish. Behind the candy counter across the aisle a young girl scooped glowing balls of candy from the bin with a brass scoop into paper bags. She..." etc., etc. At other times I tried in this same notebook to begin a short story: "Everywhere he went in the city he heard the clicking of typewriters. He woke sometimes at night from dreams of terrible violence. Lying trembling in bed, he..." etc. But it all came to nothing. I told myself that if I wrote faithfully in my notebook, not fiction, simply descriptions, in some mysterious way my inability to write something sustained and truthful would be short-circuited. In the pages about the young man who heard typewriters clicking everywhere, I wrote: "He tells himself that if he lies still long enough, his lassitude will be accomplished," but what I meant was if he stopped struggling he would be able to write just like all the unseen writers all over the city who were responsible for the clicking that was driving him mad with chagrin.

Nevertheless, despite the fact that I had nothing to write about but not writing, I put great stock, in conversation at least, in the notion of work, and my friends and I talked a good deal about our "work." "Are you working?" we asked one another. "I am trying to get to work," we said. "I am having trouble working," we said. Talking like this seemed a part of working, it was the next best thing.

We thought work should have no goal other than the doing of the thing itself. You should go to your work daily, to your desk or your table, and put in your hours. To think about a product, a finished piece of work, was a sign of banality. Anything that developed from your hours of work, a story, an article, was incidental. To be concerned with results was the mark of an ordinary person, someone with his eyes on worldly things. We adopted Stavros's and Elena's expression, "shoemakers and priests." We were priests, all four of us; Elena and I, writers; Richard and Stavros, philosophers. Shoemakers were supposed artists, supposed philosophers, who performed their sacred task as though it was an ordinary activity. Like a shoemaker who clasps a pump against his apron as he pries shank from heel, these do their work without raising their eyes to the horizon. We knew many such; we loved to classify the other graduate students, other writers, painters, and teachers, as priests or shoemakers.

There were other things that made me feel priestlike: staying up very late, preferably all night, talking; smoking a lot, and using a wooden bowl as big as a soup bowl for an ashtray, like Elena; writing telephone numbers on the wall over the phone, like Stavros; like Elena, slicing scallions on the bias. We wanted to eliminate the trivial, the mild, from our lives. Elena told me Americans were trivial, were always cheerful, always smiling. I tried not to smile. I wanted to Europeanize myself.

Stavros and Elena both had serious raincoats. Elena wore hers all the time. Except for her raincoat, her clothes were all black. Once, she and I, walking somewhere south of Houston Street, turned a corner and walked straight into a little knot of teenaged boys, who called out, "Hey, lady, how's the spy business?" I knew they were making fun of her raincoat. She had dark brown hair knotted low at the back of her neck and a pale oval face. Her hands were stubby and her fingers stained with tobacco. She taught me to say, in Greek, "The child plays on the seashore." She drank Scotch, neat. She loved cheese Danish. She sang Turkish songs.

Elena wrote a story which opened: "The priest wore a skirt, but Iphigenia could see, if she lay on her stomach, that under the skirt he wore trousers." She read the story out loud to us, pronouncing "skirt" "skeert," and "stomach" "stow-mach." I was moved to envy. She wrote another story, called "The Masked Ball," somewhat in the style of Fielding, with long sentences not quite perfect in syntax, heavy with irony and sagging with Homeric similes. In the story, after having expended much thought and anxiety over his costume, the hero, upon arriving at the loft where the party was in progress, slips and falls backward down the stairs, injuring himself sufficiently badly as to make it impossible for him to attend the party. It made me ashamed of my own efforts. I tried to develop an armored style and to choose a subject that was objectively interesting. Like all writers, I wanted to write something serious and funny, something complex and at the same time simple, something that would win the admiration of my friends and set my anxiety about myself to rest. But it was too difficult. I went back to my notebook, describing the weather, referring obliquely to events in my psychoanalysis, and remarking to myself that writing was getting easier all the time.

As we labored to show that we were priestlike in our work, so also about sex we wanted to have a priestly attitude. Together with Elena and Stavros we talked about having what we called an orgy. Our plans, however, had more of a doctrinal than an erotic cast. We wished, I believe, to mount some sexual performance that would confer upon us all the imprimatur of the chosen. We spoke about casting off from the shores of ordinary morality and setting out without the restraints we had been brought up within, restraints necessary, no doubt, for those who did not seek to widen their understanding, but confining for the artist or the explorer. We discussed at length setting, nuance, accoutrements. At last we decided we were ready to stage the thing itself. I remember, but not too well, my

husband and myself attempting to have sexual intercourse
on the floor of our apartment on East 17th Street, in the
half-dark, with Elena and Stavros similarly occupied a short
distance away. We believed ourselves to be shattering an
awesome taboo and that in so doing a great liberty would
be available to us. Perhaps all my difficulties in writing
stories would be swept away. The following morning, in
the subway on my way to Harper & Brothers, where I
was a secretary in the children's book department, I looked
around at the car full of men and women going to work,
and I felt set apart.

When we were taken to see our summer house for the
first time—the house that was going to be ours, that is—
it was a still, humid August afternoon. It was a good house,
the agent told us, an eighteenth-century house, but it needed
a little work. It had just come on the market; we were the
first to see it. The agent was a big man, wearing a short-
sleeved shirt. His tan gabardine jacket was folded over the
front seat between him and Richard. As he drove smoothly
through the exhausted countryside, he explained that the
children of the owners had decided the house must be sold,
but since they knew their father would be bound to object,
a small deception would have to be practiced. We were to
be looking at the house as prospective renters, he told us,
and merely as possible prospective renters at that, should
the old man decide to spend the winter in Florida for his
health. That was the story to get us in to see the house.
The children would find a way to deal with his objections
if and when we showed an interest. We were to have no
lines to say in this drama; we had only to stand by while
the agent spun off his part.

The paved road became a dirt road, climbed a short
way through hemlock woods, emerged and ran between
untended fields yellow with goldenrod. We passed a maple tree with one red branch. Beside the road the sumac

was already streaked with lavender. A pickup truck approached us, raising a cloud of dust. The agent pulled to the side of the road and we quickly closed the car windows. We opened them at once; the heat in the closed car was stifling.

"Alrighty," said the agent. He turned into a short drive and stopped. We got out, blinking in the sun. The agent waited, running his handkerchief over his forehead, while we looked at the outside of the house, the sagging roof, the peeling paint, the overgrown garden. A single hollyhock, tall as a grown person, unstaked, with flowers the color of plums and leaves eaten to lace by Japanese beetles, swayed in the hot breeze.

"Oh, she had quite a garden," said the agent. "Quite a garden. She's English. You could bring it back. It's not too far gone."

He stood on the front step and knocked on the door. Turning to us standing below on the grass, he said, "She can't hear. Won't wear a hearing aid, but can't hear." He banged the door with his fist, then pushed it open. "Hello-o-o? Mrs. Bailey? Hello-o-o." He put his head in the door. "They have the TV on, besides. Come on."

Inside, the house was dark. Green shades in all the windows were drawn against the sun except in the lower half of one where a square fan stirred a warm flow of air. A smell, sharp and sweet both, struck me and I had to swallow once and then again. It was medicine I smelled, medicine and talcum powder, and perhaps urine, as well. The old man was sitting in his pajamas, in a woolen plaid bathrobe, pink-skinned, with fine silvery hair, asleep. There was a bed in the room, brought from somewhere else, I thought, because it took up more than half of the space. The other furniture was crowded together at the far end of the room. Mrs. Bailey, who had been looking at television, smoking, turned her head as we entered and looked at us with no expression at all for a minute. Then she composed her features, pursed her lips, and smiled. Putting her hands on the arms of the chair, she tried to stand up quickly but dropped her cigarette and reached down for it.

The agent stepped forward while we stood decorously in the doorway.

"Mrs. Bailey," he said, "good to see you. Not too hot for you?"

"Oh, Tom," she said, "yes, indeed. But the fan makes a glorious breeze, don't you think?" She was deeply lined, thin, heavily rouged, with black circles under her eyes. Seeing us, she cocked her head to one side and looked up at him with an artificial, questioning expression.

"These are the people who are interested in taking a look at the house." He introduced us and I shook her cold hand. Cigarette ashes fell down the front of her dress. She looked down and impatiently brushed them away. "Well, come on," she said, "have a look." She was attempting with trembling hands to light another cigarette. Tom, the agent, bent over her with his hands cupped around his lighter while she inhaled greedily.

I glanced at the old man, who was moving in his armchair, waking up. He turned his head from side to side, smacking his lips, muttering.

"How are you, Mr. Bailey?" shouted the agent. "We came to see you."

"I'm eighty-four years old," he said to us. "Imagine that. I never thought. Hello, Tommy," he said, recognizing the agent. "Come to see the house?" He didn't look suspicious in the least, I thought. On the contrary, he smiled sweetly, then sighed and held his hands out in front of him, fingers extended, looked at them, and put them down in his lap. He looked straight at me. His eyes were light blue. "Go on," he said to the agent. "Go on, show them around."

But as we stepped into the hall on our way to the kitchen, he called us back. "It's called 'Green Fields.' Did you know that, Tommy? That's what I named it way back when. All right, go on."

"That's nice," said the agent. "'Green Fields.' No, I didn't know that. Very nice."

In the kitchen Mrs. Bailey lifted a lid from the coal stove and threw in her cigarette.

"Let me show you," she said, and unfolded a sheet of glossy paper which she spread out on the table. "It's the plans for the condo." She explained that she and her daughter, not Mr. Bailey's daughter but the one that was hers and not his, were going to live together in New Jersey. "That's my daughter I had when I was married in England," she said. "Do you see that?" she asked, pointing to a framed photograph of a stone house surrounded with roses. "That's my garden. I had everything growing there. Absolutely everything. People came from everywhere to see it." She shook her head. "He really has to go," she said. "I cannot manage another winter here with him. There were days in a row when no one could get up or down the road." She turned to me and said, "It was under ten for two weeks. Under ten below, I mean to say. I can't manage it again. It's impossible for someone used to the climate in Devon." She smiled at us and waved her hands in a way I understood was intended to evoke for us the gentle air of the west of England. The agent, in an effort to soften her indictment of the harshness of the winters, began to say something about cross-country skiing in a casual voice. Mrs. Bailey coughed, a long cough. She stood there, coughing, with one hand against the wall. At length, she caught her breath and tottered around with us from room to room, leaving little ridges and droppings of ash in her wake. She knew all about the behind-the-scenes plan, it seemed; clearly, she had been present at the councils.

In the bedroom, Richard and I exchanged a look which meant that despite the condition of the house we wanted it. The price was low, we should make an offer, we should buy it. We would sweep out the traces of the Baileys and everyone who had fumbled there before us. We would tear

down the false moldings and plywood partitions, rip up
the worn floorboards, burn the carpets with their scorches
and stains. Our house would be fresh and cool in the summer. In winter, firelight would shine on the waxed floor.

Then, by early October, the Baileys were gone. He was
taken to a nursing home in Connecticut, near the daughter
that was his, and she, ill, to the hospital in Springfield.
The house was ours, empty, smelling of autumn mold and
human effluvia. We opened all the doors and windows and
walked from room to room considering what best to do.
Then we turned our attention to setting in motion the plans
we had decided upon in the matter of repairs and resto-
ration, of choosing workmen, building a center chimney,
installing twelve-over-twelve windows, putting down new
pine floors, replacing the asphalt roof with cedar shingles,
and buying the new kitchen appliances, the new tiles and
faucets for the bathroom, and the new gleaming pink copper pipes to replace the plumbing in the whole house.

Driving Back
from the Funeral

❧ ❧

❧ ❧ Driving back from the funeral in Harrisburg, we took a route that cut through coal-mining country. Snow was forecast in the west, and as we started into the hills we saw snow in the fields. As we climbed, the snow grew deeper, and after a while it crept out of the fields onto the shoulders of the road. Where the road was in shadow, there were patches of ice. We passed through no villages or towns.

With the romanticism of a city person, I was looking for the rural picturesque, the neat field, the pleasing demarcation of meadow and woods. The road was straight and followed the top of the ridge. Fields sloped away on either side. From time to time the slope extended so far down that even if I leaned my cheek against the side window I couldn't see the bottom, only the slope rising on the far side. I surveyed the landscape for a farmhouse set just so within the white rectangles of the farmyard. I was looking for some man-made construction—shed, barn, silo—the comforting evidence of a rural past. But there were no farms. The fields were lumpy, and trees poked the sky at strange angles. The covering of snow, which here and there deepened to drifts, masked but did not conceal the irregularities beneath the surface of the ground.

It was not until I saw the first cone and thought at once, Slag heap, that I understood where we were. "Slag heap," said my husband. As we were passing the first, others emerged from behind. The character of the landscape had changed. The hint of something distressing had solidified into a fact. Why did we come this way? I thought. This wasn't going to be fun.

We sat in silence. My husband drove. Above the snowy hillsides white hills rose; beyond them, a white sky. Perhaps we were not going to escape the new snowstorm. We were driving a little too fast, considering the snowbanks crowding the road and the slippery patches and the cars in our lane and in the other, driving too fast themselves and subtly urging us to keep up.

We sped along, curving with the curves of the highway. I turned on the radio and tried up and down the dial to find something for us to listen to, but after a while I switched it off and sat back. At once, the silence between us swelled. It would not be muffled by the sound of the tires on the pavement, of the engine accelerating and slowing, by the clicking of the turn signal or the flashlight rolling in the glove compartment. In it, my thoughts followed with the tail of one stuck in the jaws of the one behind. My thoughts were so thick that to isolate one you would have had to unravel the whole. They made a terrific din in my head. But they refused to be translated into speech.

Perhaps in my husband's head a parallel loom clattered. No doubt it did. I have on occasion, on other drives, for instance, asked him, "What are you thinking about?" And he would answer, "I was calculating the mileage," or "I hear a little knock when you accelerate. There, do you hear it?" Now I leaned away from him against the armrest and closed my eyes. What might span our two silences? What would I say if he asked me what I was thinking about?

"Oh, look!" I said. "Look at the little stairway going all the way to the top of the slag heap. It's so delicate. Like twigs in the snow."

And responding no doubt to the foolishness of my remark, my husband said nothing.

We drove on.

The evening before, just at dark, while we were parking, my husband's sister had said, "I'm worried about the funeral parlor. People told me it's the right one to use, but it seems so dingy."

On the porch of the funeral parlor, two painted metal chairs leaned with their foreheads touching the railing and their tubular stands sticking up behind. Summer chairs. We stood on the porch and looked out to the street. The traffic was sparse, but what cars there were rushed past as if they were on a highway. Across, in a window, a blue sign read ALTER-ATIONS. Perhaps it was that sign that distressed my sister-in-law. Inside, the funeral parlor was not at all dingy. It had wooden walls varnished golden brown. Lamps shone through milk-glass globes. The front room, where the dead man lay, was brightly lit. He was himself brightly lit, as if by a spotlight; his satin pillow shone and his wedding ring gleamed. Large bunches of funeral flowers rose in tiers from the floor to the casket: white chrysanthemums, white and yellow gladiolas, yellow roses. I bent my head to smell the roses but then raised it instead, checked by the sight of the dead man's white nose and sculptured lips.

Standing beside the body, my sister-in-law asked us if we didn't think Mr. Gray, the undertaker, who was nodding to us respectfully from the doorway, was to be congratulated. I understood that she felt some obligation to be gracious to him. I had never met my sister-in-law's husband, to whom she had been only briefly married, but my husband, who had, said he looked very natural and lifelike indeed. This must have cost him a lot to say, since the dead man did not look at all lifelike, but nonetheless it was well received. I, in turn, said the flowers were beautiful and beautifully arranged. "How many there are!" I said. Mr. Gray said, "They keep well in here. We keep it nice and cool, you know."

The dead man's sister, named Davida, a tall woman, somewhat heavy, with strong eyebrows, came in through a door at the back. "I parked behind the house," she said. We shook hands. Her hand was large and her handshake was energetic. She had the same large features as her brother. Sitting on the edge of a chair, she pulled off her galoshes. "More snow on the way," she said. "Well," she said to my husband, standing up and pushing her scarf into her sleeve, "it's good to see you fellows. You didn't come down for Thanksgiving." Having hung up her overcoat and set her galoshes on the floor under the coat tree, she went in to look at the body. I saw her dark silhouette against the casket.

"Well," she said, as she turned around and came toward us, hands extended palms up, as though to say, There's nothing to do about it, is there?

Then we stood beside the body. He seemed to be demanding something of me, of us all, but I didn't know what it was. Every now and then tears would leak into my eyes. But I was not at all sad. In that cold white light there was something imperious about him. What did he want of us? Did he want us to weep? I wanted to look at him, and yet I didn't in the least want to look. Did I think it was shameful? Or was it fear that held me back? I walked back and forth. Something was pressing me to be animated, to be friendly, to move quickly about the room noting a sepia engraving here, there a ceramic spittoon. I couldn't stop moving.

At length we sat down in the foyer. Our four chairs were arranged in a square. Our ankles and feet nearly met. I was aware of our dark shoes and stockings, moving and shifting as we talked. Next to us the varnished stairway led upstairs. From where I was sitting I could see obliquely into the room where the dead man lay; his two black shoes were visible.

My sister-in-law and Davida took out their cigarettes and matches, and my sister-in-law got up to get ashtrays, but Mr. Gray anticipated her. We began to talk. I asked Davida where she lived, and she said she had lived all her life just outside Harrisburg but she was thinking about moving.

"I could live anywhere now," she said. "Now that I've got my children grown. My baby's just got her driver's license."

"Oh, my," said my sister-in-law. She smiled at Davida. Then she looked around. Perhaps she was wondering if anyone else was coming. She was the hostess here, in a way. In a way, though, Mr. Gray was the host. In another way, I felt I was, and so I said to Davida, "Would you go somewhere you have friends?"

"I make friends quickly," she said.

"Oh, she does, like a shot." My sister-in-law laughed and then stopped laughing at a sound from the back of the house. She listened and turned to my husband. "Davida's a doctor too, you know," she said. "She's a veterinarian."

"I remember," my husband said. "You told me that when you and Bob got married." We all looked up, even my husband, at the sound of the dead man's name. There was a silence. Both Davida and my sister-in-law started to speak, but the door opened and in came Davida's two daughters. Having kissed their mother and their aunt, who introduced them to me, they shook hands with Mr. Gray and sat down on the folding chairs he had hurried to bring. They had pale perfect skin and brownish-yellow eyes. A third daughter, the youngest of the children, the one who had just got her driver's license, had stayed at home, they said, because she was upset. They explained she had felt ill at supper, remembering her father's funeral. Their father, they told me, had died last year.

Oh, I thought, then they are getting used to it. What were they all feeling? If they were in fact getting used to it, why was the youngest alone at home instead of here with us? Was it the thought of her father lying in his grave while she was eating her supper that had made her ill? She could not come to see her dead uncle. That would be too painful. Perhaps it was because she was so young, really a child still, despite her new license. Her sisters did not seem upset. They were calm and cheerful and polite to me, whom they had never met. To their mother they were quietly affectionate. My sister-in-law was also cheerful and attentive, fetching ashtrays and making introductions. Although strained, she was not distraught. Her eyes were tired and wary, but they were not red. She seemed glad when there was something to smile over.

"I have to decide what to do about Bob's things," she said to us all. "His car, for one thing."

"Oh," said Davida. "Do you mean the Plymouth? Does he still have that?"

The elder of the girls frowned at the present tense.

"My lord!" Davida went on. "I remember his first one. That was a terror. Mama was in a panic he'd kill himself." There was a silence. Davida spoke again. "Well, you'd best be satisfied not getting too much for it. There's no market these days. Not even for secondhand. Don't I know it! It will keep you busy for quite a time. Selling things."

We all thought about money then. And about selling the things his wife wouldn't keep and how much, or how little, she would get for them. Then we burst into a conversation about inflation, about taxes, about salaries, jobs, and social security. Several people unknown to me had come in, had stood beside the body, spoken to my sister-in-law, to Davida, the girls. There was a pleasant decorous feeling in the room and a pleasant murmur of voices.

But at length we stood up and said good night. In a meaningful way, we said we would see one another in the morning. That meant here at the funeral. We stood in three groups: my husband and myself, Davida and her daughters, and my sister-in-law. We embraced. We all shook hands with Mr. Gray and Miss Gray, his pale sister, who had appeared and smiled at us and had begun to turn the lamps off, one by one.

My sister-in-law apologized to Mr. Gray lest we had stayed too long. With her coat on and her scarf in her hand, she went back into the front room and stood next to her husband. She didn't touch him but she bent near him and seemed to say something.

Then, dressed in overcoats and boots, gloves, mittens, and scarves, we crowded into the hall and thence to the cold night air, while Mr. Gray closed the door firmly behind us.

We drove my sister-in-law home and said we would not come in. In our motel room we looked at television before we went to sleep. I slept heavily for part of the night but then woke and lay awake in the dark room. After quite a long while, I got out of bed and pulled apart the heavy rubberized curtains so I could see the night sky.

At the funeral I sat in the front. The casket was closed and upon it rested two vases of spiky flowers. Behind me I heard the little rustlings and creakings of the mourners. Nearby I could see Mr. Gray, in an alcove at the side of the room, standing close to the wall with his face turned toward the minister. There was a dimmer on the wall with two dials, and Mr. Gray kept a hand on each. The minister spoke. "O, Death," he said, "brother of Sleep...." The light on the casket faded to a glow and thence to near darkness, as Mr. Gray made a series of minute adjustments, all the while listening attentively as the minister spoke of the calm which follows strife and the peace we know not of. He mentioned thrones, gardens and rivers, dust, of course, ashes and garments, the kingdom of this world and the city of heaven. At last his voice signaled by a change of tone that he was coming to the end.

"Good night, sweet prince," he said, and a column of light fell from over his head and made a shiny circle on the casket between the flowers, "and flights of angels sing thee to thy rest." I might have had to restrain myself from smiling at that triumphantly produced column of light and the burst of organ notes that was so well synchronized with it, at the hands, no doubt, of Miss Gray, at her instrument at the back, hidden behind some fold of velvet in her dim alcove, but instead my eyes stung. I wiped them with my hand and wondered who I was crying for; as much for anyone, it seemed, as for anyone else. Taking a cue from the minister's anthology, I said to myself, "If you have tears . . . ," and then leafed on to ". . . it tolls for Thee," but quickly I closed the book on irony.

It was a long drive. I leaned my head against the headrest. The map slid from my lap and covered my legs. I left it there. Through half-closed eyes I watched the world rush past. Suddenly I saw something that made me sit up straight and look back. "Oh," I cried out loud, without meaning to. What I had seen was a sort of house, a sort of shed, painted dark green or black, set a little back from the road. Around the front and along one side was a concrete apron, with cars parked on it. Inside, there must have been a forge, or a big fireplace with a fire in it, because an unsteady light like firelight had flickered at the windows. I thought I saw people sitting at a table. Outside, a big dog on a chain attached to the door at the side strained and leaped to see in the high window. His legs splayed against the door at the top of his leap and then he slid down to the concrete, where he gathered his strength and hurled himself again.

"What?" said my husband. "What is it? Do you want me to go back?"

I was still twisted around. The figure of the dog, at my last look, was like a big brown animal skin pinned to the door. It was nothing, I told my husband. Something I saw. Something I thought I saw.

I must have turned around in a strange way, however, because a few minutes later my husband said, "I couldn't stop there. We were going too fast to stop without warning." I didn't want him to go back. All I had seen was a house with people inside and a dog trying to see in, or get in.

I closed my eyes. I was floating. Behind my closed eyes, I saw the house where the people had gathered. At once I assigned to them a funeral of their own. Surely the parked cars showed that they had gathered for obsequies. Sliding in and out of sleep, I provided them a corpse. They were bending over the body in firelight; it was part of their ritual. One person at a time drew close. Leaning down, he kissed the mouth and then moved away to make way for the next in line. The line snaked; there were many people. I heard the sound of bare feet and smelled damp wool. Shadows staggered on the wall as the fire rose and fell. Beneath the house was the passage through which, at the proper time, the body would be lowered. I understood that the earth was riddled with tunnels. Deep underground the bodies of men and of animals had to leak away their fluids before their dry parts could flake to earth.

In the funeral home I had prowled about, looked attentively at pictures, carpets, floors, walls, noted the lamps, the flowers, seen his ring and his shoes. I had looked quickly into the faces of his wife and his sister.

At the funeral I sat next to my husband. My eyes had stung. But what was it that made them sting? Not sorrow. No, it was not sorrow. What does death say to the living? In the face of death, do not our grievances fall away? They do and they do not. True, as I stood beside the dead man, my stubborn heart was silenced at the sight of his white nose, his curved lips, but the silence lasted for only a minute, and then the lesson was lost. What lesson do I mean? That in the presence of death the little rages of the heart must scatter. Looking at him I thought, We are in death's presence, and so I resolved to be tender forever. But of its own accord the chatter started again, and I was as before.

Once before, in the past, illness had spoken sharply to

me and I had listened, but then as now before long the words were lost and I heard nothing. Five years ago, when I had been married for five years, my husband telephoned from a colleague's office. He said they thought it was likely he had a melanoma. It's a serious business, he said. I couldn't speak, but he said rather quickly that everything had already been set in motion. The appropriate steps would have to be taken. We had nothing to do but wait our turn. "It's a serious business," he said again, "but don't worry." I said I would not worry.

I sat down on our bed. Shortly, the telephone began to buzz and I looked down to see I had not set the receiver properly in its cradle. When I had adjusted the receiver, I looked around the bedroom. And everything was altered. In the moment between fixing the telephone and raising my head, what had been noisy and complicated became simple. Death had pulled himself to his feet and stood over me. In my heart, doors leading to unexpected consequences flew open, and tenderness, unexpectedly, in the space of a few minutes, was given to me.

The days that followed were clear and sweet. Before, our two selves, scabby, each rubbed raw by the other, had been grotesquely willful and withdrawn. Now fear acted upon us as an abrasive and smoothed our scars. Our wills were returned to us and our souls were rational, tender, and clear.

But all the while, underneath, I heard a cracked voice muttering, "Won't last," as though an old woman, coming out of the dark, squinting at the sky, was cackling, "Won't last, can't last." Whether she spoke in wisdom, kindness, or malice, I couldn't say, but she knew that despite the moments of delay while the nest is spared or the furrow made crooked to let the columbine stand, in the long run it comes to the same. The great wheel turns and turns and tumbles the blossoms with the straw, and it doesn't matter whether love is renewed before the blow. But it seems to matter. It matters.

Although my eyes were still closed, I was wide awake.
I heard my husband shifting gears, moving his hands on
the steering wheel, his foot on the accelerator. I could hear
his sleeve brushing against the body of his overcoat. Now
that I had started to listen, I heard many little sounds from
his throat, his lips, his chest. He drew a deep breath, cleared
his throat, sighed. Perhaps my isolation was willful. If it
was, then that was a sin, of sorts. To put my thoughts
into words and to speak these words out loud should not
be impossible.

"Where are we now?" I asked, sitting up.

"We've gone about ninety miles," he said. "Ninety-three,
to be exact. You were sleeping."

"Yes," I said. "No. I was thinking."

"About what?" he asked, after a short silence.

Then it was my turn to hesitate before I answered.
"Davida. And your sister. And the funeral parlor." I couldn't
seem to go beyond naming people and things.

We drove on a short way, then stopped before an old
farmhouse in front of which two gas pumps stood, not
entirely upright, with snowy helmets on top. The house
was partially hidden by heaps of snow mounded by the
plows. The skeleton of a barn clattered in the wind. Snow
was blowing off the fields in swirls.

My husband got out and peered here and there for a
gauge to check the pressure of one of the front tires, but
it was clear that if there was a pressure gauge in this gas
station, which did not seem to be functioning any more,
it was under the snow. I got out to stretch and as I walked
around the car I saw a face at the window, an old woman's
face. "Look there, in the window," I said. Clearly, this was
no longer a gas station. She had probably forgotten that
the gas pumps invited travelers and was watching us ap-
prehensively. You can't trust people any more, she was
thinking. My husband pantomimed to her that we were
merely looking for the pressure gauge but she looked
alarmed and dropped the curtain. "We can't just drive

away," he said and climbed the front step. I followed.

The old woman opened the door a crack. Then she opened the door wide. Standing beside her, a country dog looked up at us. "Come right in," she said. "I have a telephone. Is that what you were looking for?"

I had imagined our encounter could take place with us outside and her in the doorway, but it wasn't like that; we were motioned in and we had to go in.

I had seen at once there was something wrong with the old woman's nose. It was that that made us have to go in. Otherwise we could have talked to her from the doorstep, in the windy snow. Inside, the light green paint on the walls was crazed in a system of black wirelike lines, and flakes of green paint lay on the floor. Magazines were piled neatly on a couch and on a wooden bench. The kitchen stove had been pulled away from the wall, as had the refrigerator. They stood together in the middle of the room with their doors standing open. The old woman made her way back to a little table. On it stood a glass of pinkish water with a teaspoon standing up in it. Beside the glass was a dish with the peel of an orange and a bit of a pear. But the old lady herself was growing something on her nose, something garnet-colored, with many tiny gouts, or lobes. In profile I saw that the bridge of her nose was missing, and that the growth waxed intricately where the bridge of her nose had been. I couldn't tell from the look of it whether it was scabby or smooth.

"Well, come and sit down," she said, and we did, across from her at the little table with the dish and the glass, the fruit peelings and two knives. I sat down as an alternative to running out into the snow. After all, it's only something human, I thought. What can happen? I can stand looking at it. It was a sort of test. But it wasn't really a test, because I knew I could pass it.

"Well, I am glad you came to the door," she said. "I do get concerned when someone stops and I don't know who they are. Not that many stop now." The yellow dog, having ceased to sniff us, lay down noisily at her feet. He didn't close his eyes, but kept watching us.

"We didn't want to frighten you," said my husband.

"I have had so much trouble," said the old woman, and I thought she was going to tell us about her nose, but instead she told us about the rats, how she had heard a drumming and a sound from the cellar like the sea, or a wind, or a pack of wild animals. She had waked up in the night and gone to the cellar door and looked down and there they were. "One climbing upon the other, twisting all about, weaving themselves together and apart. They were like a river. And big, big as cats. They tore up all the insulation, you know, out from the walls and knocked the pickles off the shelves. And they ripped into the sack of warfarin—you know, the poison—and rushed out into the snow to die. But it took them days. There were hordes of them. I counted forty dead ones myself alone."

All the time I thought it was going to have something to do with her nose, that the rats had bitten her nose, that she was going to tell us how this army had tumbled around her and leaped up and attacked her, biting and clawing, but she didn't say anything about her nose at all. She repeated the story, emphasizing how they had come in a pack, tearing across the fields, and how they had plunged in the night down into her basement and there had rioted night after night, dying of her poison and wildly rampaging through her insulation.

"Well, they're gone now." I wondered when this had happened. Just now? Or years ago. Behind her wire glasses, her two eyelids curved smoothly. Light from the window crept under her glasses and rested upon her fuzzy cheek. In that simple light her growth glowed the color of resin. Was it a beacon before her all the days of her life? Did she ever touch it? It was right before her eyes. Was that why she had closed them? Did she see it before her? Or did she look past it, to the tufts of torn insulation and the powdery wood that showed in the places where the linoleum was worn through?

On the far wall was a bookcase, full of books lying in piles, dark books. Curiosity rose in me. Perhaps we had come upon a treasure.

Cunning, informed by avarice, spoke. "Were you a teacher?" I asked.

"Yes, I was. For fifty years. I was a teacher for fifty years."

"I thought you might have been a teacher," I said. "You speak so well."

"Yes," said the old woman. "I taught at the old Bible school. I taught scripture."

Bibles, I thought. Bibles and pamphlets. Not what I wanted.

Now it seemed perfectly easy to stand up and thank the old lady and say we didn't really need to telephone and say good-bye and go.

In the car my husband said, "Forget about the tire. It isn't anything that can't wait." Then he said, "Basal cell carcinoma."

"Is that what it is?"

"Very likely. A slow riot of cells."

I glanced sidewise at him to see if he looked distressed. Distressed at the thought of that slow riot that leaves the body porous. Papery and run through with holes, wind blowing through. The riot that mounds garnets on the nose and grapes in the brain. But he did not look distressed. He looked calm and as though he was glad to be driving again. I looked straight ahead, but I was aware that he turned his head for an instant to look at me. Then he turned his eyes back to the road. Nothing will happen now, I thought heavily, nothing. We will get home, and put the car away, and maybe go out to eat, and go to bed. And tomorrow. And the next day. There was nothing to think about. I decided to sleep.

Because my eyes were closed, I felt the beginning of the skid before I saw that the cars ahead of us had stopped. At the same moment I felt us begin to skid I heard my husband grunt, and from then on I concentrated wholly on an obscure meditation, in which it seemed that only by rendering myself completely passive could I hope to contribute to our eventual safety.

"OK," said my husband softly. "Hold on now."

Before us the gray side of a trailer truck extended across the highway. The surface of the road showed the waves of large tire marks, as well as the thinner skid marks of the cars as they braked to avoid the trailer. We were sliding over the road, turning first one side and then the other to the looming truck, whose cab, like the head of a grazing beast, seemed to contemplate our approach. All right, I thought, it ends here. Fear held me still. A noise came out of my mouth, not a scream, just a breath, but even before we came to a stop the diminishing curves of our skid told me it was going to be all right, we were not going to die. When we stopped, we were completely turned around, facing Harrisburg.

Tears jumped to my eyes, stood, bulged, and tumbled over. I felt all that with pleasure, the sting of my tears, the fullness.

My husband rested one hand upon mine. Then we undid our seat belts and put our arms around one another. I felt his beard against my cheek and the soft part of his neck where the beard stops. His heart was beating heavily. I felt it as well as my own. In my body that solid fear eased and began to slide away. It would have been nice to stay there, not to move. Having given ourselves up for lost, having folded my hands and said, "Lord, take me," why not consider the rest of our lives a serendipity, a gift?

But after a time we refastened our seat belts, and my husband restarted the car. Extending his arm across the back of my seat, he twisted far around to see behind us while he maneuvered us back into our lane, edging past the corner of the truck and between the cars and setting us once more on our way.

There is a certain beautiful light seen sometimes at the seaside in the evening after the sun has set, when the sky, although still retaining some color, is darker than the sea. At such moments, the water may be the lightest green or turquoise, and the sky quivers above it. Beauty and light stream upward as the sea that has rocked comfortably under the blaze of day returns a submerged radiance to the darkening sky. So the snowy fields on the hilltops seemed joined to the sky as we resumed our interrupted journey. Quick winter evening was rushing toward us. We were driving away from where the sun had set toward the darker part of the sky.

My husband spoke: "I wonder if she realized she wouldn't see him again."

I understood he was speaking of the moment when his sister had stood beside the body of her husband, holding her pocketbook and her gloves and her orange scarf, before we all left the funeral parlor and Mr. Gray had locked up behind us and we had driven her home for the night.

"I couldn't look at him enough," I said. "I would look and then look away." As if there were something to stare down, as if there were something to achieve by this looking, something to win.

A Summer's
Day

𝕽 𝕽 Daniel Stern sat down at one of the small tables under the awning on the court side of the clubhouse. He balanced his tennis racket against the leg of the opposite chair and on its seat he set his can of balls. He was saving the chair for his wife, Judith, whose doubles game, he could see, was in its last set. His own game had been satisfying. He had won one set with what was perhaps the best tennis he had ever played, starting with the return of a virtually unreturnable service and ending with a short, hard crosscourt shot that had taken the point. Could Judith have seen it? He hoped she had been looking.

He stretched his shoulders and ran his hands along his forearms. Looking down at his muscular, compact legs, he tensed his calves, then let them relax. He took a sip from the plastic cup on the table in front of him.

It was August, the middle of the morning. On the lawn, under a bright sun, cut grass lay drying in white lines. Behind him, in the dim light of the clubhouse, men were signing up to play later in the day. Others, finished playing, turned from the bar, balancing their cold drinks, as they considered where to sit. He greeted them by name in a pleasant neutral voice: "Bob," he said, "Peter." And they answered in kind: "Dan."

He turned his chair to watch the tennis, but after a minute felt a hand on his shoulder. "Dan? How about one more?"

He shook his head. "No," he said. "Thanks. I had quite a workout."

Daniel was thirty-seven years old. He was a lawyer, a

partner in the firm his father had founded. His father was dead, he had died when Daniel was in law school; his mother had not remarried. He had been an only child, with an eager laugh and anxious dark eyes, fond of many grown-ups, and his teachers and camp counselors had, in turn, been fond of him. He had been small for his age and young in his class. At fifteen, the hair on his upper lip had darkened and from time to time he tried out his father's razor, but he hadn't needed to shave until he was in college. In his thirties, his beard grew heavy. Now he shaved closely in the morning and often in the evening as well. He loved to sleep late on Saturday and Sunday, and at night he fell asleep easily, with Judith beside him. Although he got on well with women, he had not been unfaithful to his wife; nor, even though he got on well with men, had he any close friends. He liked waiting at the bus stop in the morning with the newspaper under his arm, while his daughter Sarah chattered, swung her book bag, and fooled with his coat sleeve until her bus came and he kissed her and hurried to the subway. He liked going to the barber on the way to work; he liked riding the elevator up to the office. On those evenings, after the secretaries, the switchboard operator, and the girls in the typing pool had gone home, when he and Mr. Rosen or one of the other partners had taken off their jackets and hung them over the backs of their chairs, he was happy to settle in for a long night of work. After a while, one of them would stand up and say, "Can I get you something?" and bring to the table the whiskey, the ice bucket, and a siphon of soda. Sipping Scotch and soda and scooping up handfuls of peanuts while the piles of papers mounted and the pink light of evening darkened to night, Daniel would pause sometimes and reach for the phone. "Jude?" he would say. "Don't wait for me, I'm going to be late," and he would turn back to his yellow pad and the figures and notes for the task at hand, but the thought of his wife, going about her life at home, putting Sarah to bed and at length going to bed herself, to read perhaps while she waited for him, gave him the sense that his life was orderly and complete.

A warm breeze was blowing, moving the bushes on the far side of the courts, flipping over leaves to show their white undersides and bending the Queen Anne's lace to the ground. The breeze was affecting some of the players, Daniel could see, particularly the women, whose laughter had become more frequent and louder as they apologized to one another for missing easy shots.

He shifted in his canvas chair to watch the progress of his wife's set. When she served, she squared her jaw and frowned and did something with her tongue against the inside of her cheek that gave her the intent, inward look of a man shaving. She had little white tassels on her socks, and she reached for the ball for her second serve in a pocket under her tennis skirt. Few of her first serves went in. He knew how hard she was trying. It made her look almost ugly. It made him look around to see if anyone else was watching.

His wife had become hardened toward him, he could see that in the determination with which she prepared to receive service. Judith was small and dark-haired. At one time she had had long hair and been plump. She used to fret about being plump. "Fat," she would say to him, standing in front of the bedroom mirror, pouting and smiling at the same time, a self-deprecating little smile, which both asserted and denied his right to agree with her, "fat. Oh, I loathe myself." Daniel would say, "Oh, Judith, you are beautiful. To me, you are beautiful," and she would frown and say, with her eyes still on her reflection, "Oh, then you mean I am ugly to everyone else?" Then he would kiss her and they would laugh. Everything vulnerable about her, that she had been sexually timid the first years of their marriage, that she used to burst into tears after a difficult scene with the cleaning woman, that she was shy when they went to dinner parties and sometimes triumphant on the way home, had made her seem uniquely his to Daniel.

117

Her white buttocks and the unsuntanned part of her abdomen had been an emblem of what was his to look at and no one else's. But now, when he saw that the skin which had stayed white in all seasons was smoothly, defiantly brown, and that she wasn't shy at all about the puckered scar on her belly, which he had seen with horror after Sarah's birth but which had come to be a sign for him that their sexual love merited a special seal, when he saw that she now went to the beach and lay on a thin mat that matched her bikini, he knew that what had been private was no longer his at all. She had had something done to her pubic hair so that none escaped her tiny bathing suit. Now the only bright white thing about her was her blazing teeth in her brown face.

It was nearly noon. The white skirts and the little sleeveless shirts of the women were so bright he had to look away. The two cans of diet soda he had thirstily drunk when he finished playing had worked upon him to ill effect; he had continually to swallow bitter saliva. The muscles of his legs had tightened, and his damp tennis shirt was cold.

He was wretched. Had he been a child, his features would have crumpled and he would have slid down in his stroller, stiffening his body and squaring his jaw. He would have cried noisily and nothing would have helped. No tears would have wet his fierce eyes or run down his cheeks. His adults would have gathered around him, offering one solace after another, while he raged on until at last he grew calmer and nodded his warm and heavy head against his mother's shoulder, which was warm and wet with his tears, and slept.

But wretchedness was not his natural element. As a boy he had been close to his mother. When she came to kiss him good night and he saw she was dressed to go out, he held his arms tightly around her bent neck until she had to pull away to get free. But she made it into a joke. She would make him laugh and he would let go. She liked to

118

walk. She walked quickly and he ran along beside her, chattering and trying to keep up. Once, in the park after the Thanksgiving Day parade, hurrying past leafless trees under a pale sky, he said to her, "Can you say what we talked about last year?" He was eleven. "Last year?" she asked. "Last year, after the parade," he answered. She stopped walking and looked at him, puzzled. "All right," she said, realizing it was a game and she was to try to remember. "Let's see," she said. She didn't get it quite, but she came close. At other times she would say, "You know, I can see right into your head. I can see what you are thinking." And indeed, to his delight, she often could. But she could less and less as he grew older, until finally he had to wrench himself away. It took a long time but finally he got loose, blinding himself from the sight of her charming, wounded face. She had no one else. Now she lived in Florida. That was when he first met Judith, when he was at law school, in the midst of that turmoil. Judith used to come to his apartment on 112th Street, and sometimes, when he held her face between his hands and kissed her lips, he could feel his life turning around. Once he saw tears running down her cheeks. He had been startled. "I feel so lonely," she said. She said it quite forcefully, but at the same time she smiled and even laughed in an embarrassed way. He did not know what she meant or why she had been silently crying.

Daniel was sunk far down in his canvas chair so absorbed in thoughts and dark feelings that he wasn't watching when Judith's set was finally finished, and so the women walked off the court and crossed the lawn and were standing in front of him before he saw them. He looked up and they loomed enormous. They were a crowd; how many women were there and how big were they? Their flesh was marble-like and their clothing greenish white in the green shade of the clubhouse, and they carried who knows what implements; what were they brandishing? They were chattering and hissing with laughter at him, who hadn't even seen their smiles or heard their Hi, Dan's! as they swarmed across the lawn. But in one second, in half a second, he had recovered himself and he jumped up so they wouldn't be towering over him. Next to him, Carol, Judith's partner, had her arms bent behind her head while she fingered the clasp of her necklace. Her face was darkly tanned and she frowned. "Here, Jude," she said to Judith, "you do it," and she turned her back to Judith, who slid the tongue of the clasp into the groove.

"There," said Judith with satisfaction. "You really are sweaty. Your hair is running with sweat."

"Oh, God," said Carol, "I must reek. God. It was great." To Daniel she said, "You were just waiting? You could have gone. We would have taken her home. I know, you like to keep an eye on everything, isn't that it? Well, all right. Good-bye all. Tomorrow, then."

And she was gone.

In the car the leather seats burned. Judith trailed one hand out the window and let the hot breeze dry the webs of her sweaty fingers.

"My serve was really good today," she said. She took her gold watch out of her tennis bag and fastened it. It gleamed on her wrist. One wing of her dark hair fell forward on her cheek as she bent her head over her watch strap. Daniel turned his head to look at her. She was flushed. Under her tan her legs were rosy. Daniel noticed the large blue vein, an embarrassment to her, which emerged from under her tennis dress and made its way down her thigh, branching and branching again. He wondered if it was her period yet.

Judith sighed and stretched her legs in front of her. She rotated her feet first in one direction, then the other. "I was getting some topspin," she said. She paused and then said to him, "Did you notice?"

Daniel wanted to kiss her mouth; he thought of stopping the car and moving over and pressing down upon her lips with his, feeling her teeth behind her lips, pressing her against the leather door of the car with the force of his body.

"Carol thinks my serve is coming along," she said.

Daniel said in a soft voice that Carol was a hard number.

"Why do you say that?" Judith burst out, and then in a moment she said more stiffly, "Why do you say it? I want to know."

Daniel didn't answer. He would have liked not to go on in this direction. He had meant to say nothing about his wife's friends, but the words had escaped his lips before he had even known they were in his mouth and they would now, he knew, precipitate her rage, and his own would rise to meet it, and the smolder of anger in each of them would respond across the space between them as though he, Daniel, and she, Judith, hardly existed except to provide a veneer of dry wood and varnish for these sparks to kindle into the hot gusts of serious burning.

All around the house, tall leafy trees moving in the breeze filtered the light, which fell in a continuous green flicker. Inside, it was dark and cool. The windows and the doors were open. The little girl, Sarah, lay on a wicker couch, reading. She had been lying there for too long; she kept leaning on one elbow, then switching to the other side. She was reading *Anna Karenina*. Something wouldn't happen in it. She didn't know what it was. There was Kitty. She loved Kitty. And Anna. She thought she loved Kitty. She kept saying to herself, I love Kitty. She pressed her legs together when she read about Kitty getting ready for the ball, and how beautiful her dress was and how it was one of her good days. Anna wore black velvet and pearls. Kitty's dress was pink. Sarah would have said, if anyone had asked her what she was doing, "I'm reading *Anna Karenina*. I love it!" She twisted about on the sofa. Sometimes she stopped reading for a moment or two and rested her cheek on her brown arm. She had started to read this morning in bed, before anyone was up. She had heard the sounds of her parents rising, her mother and then her father; she had heard them moving about, going downstairs, making noises in the kitchen, running water, closing doors. She was reading when she heard the car doors slam and they drove off.

Now the house was silent, it was almost lunchtime. The black kitten jumped up onto the couch beside her and she stroked his head with one hand. She raised her head and looked off into space. Then she lowered her eyes and bent her head back to the book. Which one was better, Anna or Kitty? It seemed you had to choose. The men all faded into insignificance. She was impatient with Levin and his long conversations and his long thoughts. About Vronsky, too, there was something displeasing. Was he handsome? Was he short? Didn't it say that he was getting bald? But she didn't really try to put these worries into words. She sped on, skipping the long conversations. Perhaps Levin wasn't handsome either. There was something about his complexion. He kept looking to her as though he had once had bad skin which was better now but had left his cheeks faintly pitted and his spirits dimmed. No wonder Kitty didn't really love him. There was something about him, some obscure thing, which resembled Karenin. He was struggling to master something. Only Kitty's father, the old Prince, Tolstoy called him, wasn't forever pushing against some barrier. But he was old. So there was no one perfect for Kitty, whose self was floating up from childhood bumping gently against one character and then another, as though trying doors here and there, weak and yet determined with a determination over which she had no say. What happened, happened.

Vronsky went to the stables, talked with his man, observed his rival; all that was boring. Only when his mare looked round at him with anxious, eager, encouraging eyes did the child begin to feel something like love for him. Love and fear. She already knew. She felt the mare's sides between her own legs and trembled at the danger of their enterprise. And when Vronsky broke the back of the mare she felt a thrill of terror. She felt the horse's sides between her legs and heard a snap. All her love was with him. Anna fainting in the stands was contemptible, of no interest.

Footsteps on the floor above alerted her.

"Grandpa? Is that you, Grandpa?"

She didn't want to see him right now. She heard him start down the stairs.

"Grandpa?" He appeared at the landing. He was wearing a red-and-blue striped knit shirt. His white hair was springy and showed dark waves where he had soaked it and run his comb through it.

"Good morning, darling." The light from the window on the landing shone around his body. "It almost isn't morning any more," he said.

"I didn't know you were still here. I thought everyone was out."

Subtly, unbeknownst even to herself, she schemed to avoid a morning kiss. But this morning he didn't want to kiss her.

"I slept very late," he said. "Oh, I had such a terrible dream in the night. I didn't get back to sleep until it was light. And I slept until just now."

"It's lunchtime," she said.

"Do you want to have your lunch while I have my coffee? You could keep me company and we could have our talk about Tolstoy. Today is my last day, you know." It was he who had given her *Anna Karenina*.

"I know. No, I want to wait for them," she said, stubborn and awkward. She looked out the window at the bright noon driveway, anticipating the crackle and hiss of the little stones under the wheels of the returning car. She hoped he would be out when her mother and father came home.

But Saul was distracted. He didn't plead with her even mutely. He poured his coffee and unplugged the pot.

Standing at the kitchen counter and gazing into the garden, he took a sip, and then another, and then he put down his mug. "I'm going to walk on the beach," he said. "Do you want to come?"

She shook her head. "I want to read," she said.

He started for the door to the porch, then came back and carefully rinsed his cup and set it in the rack of the dishwasher.

"Good-bye, darling," he said to her.

"'Bye," she said.

He walked in the shade of the sycamores toward the ocean. High noon and midsummer and a fine gusty wind combined to intensify the light, and he walked gratefully under the trees. But the line of sycamores came to an end and he was cast into the glare of the naked sun. He didn't feel the way he had wanted to feel on his last morning. He loved to walk on the beach and take deep breaths to fill his chest with the pure air and let the sun bombard him with vitamin D and the pores of his skin ooze away grime and corruption. He could picture his body casting off impurities: salts, cells, lipids. He loved the long showers and the deep sleeps that followed. It was his dream which lay heavily in his body and made it hard for him to draw one of those deep breaths.

He had dreamed that he was running his hands lightly over his body and had suddenly felt that he had in his hands a woman's breasts. He looked down and indeed it was true. The breasts of a woman hung upon his chest. They were the breasts of a woman of his own age, still somewhat rounded, with dark nipples, but the flesh was chalky or dusty in color, without sheen. He was not aghast at this change in his body, but he felt a heaviness, a heavy acceptance of an unpleasant fact, a fact he stoically accepted as something he would have to deal with.

Standing at the water's edge, he looked out to the horizon. "Of course there was an element of shame," he said out loud, "but I couldn't say I was surprised." In the dream,

he had known he would have to do something, see someone, a doctor, a psychiatrist, but it was Friday, and he
knew he couldn't even make an appointment until Monday. All at once he was in a psychiatrist's waiting room,
waiting until it was Monday. The nurse was a teen-aged
child wearing a white uniform and a dark blue sweater
with white buttons. She murmured to the doctor as they
crossed the waiting room going into the doctor's office
and coming out again, getting ready to close up for the
weekend. The doctor was going skiing, his wife and children were waiting in the car outside. Saul knew it was a
Mercedes, even though he didn't actually see the car in the
dream. The doctor said a few words to him; he would let
him stay there, in the waiting room, until Monday. Saul
was grateful that the doctor, despite his urbanity and his
elaborate ski equipment, seemed to recognize that his problem was not some kind of interesting anomaly but was,
instead, a sad fact. That was the end of the upsetting dream.
It was followed by a brief dream, or a fragment of a dream,
in which he was trying to read something to Judith. He
could remember this part only with the greatest difficulty.
He was reading to her, and he looked up to see if she was
listening. That was all. And then, for an instant before he
awoke, he saw the face of his dead wife. Her mouth was
open as though she had just drawn a breath and was about
to speak. But before she could say anything, he awoke.

Where were her parents? The sun was straight overhead.
It was time for them to be back. Sarah decided to set the
table for lunch, but when she was done they still had not
come. She went out to pick flowers for the table.

At the back of the garden the little pond had a scraggly
look. From the house, the flowers at the edge looked pretty,
but when she got close, she couldn't find a good flower.
She picked two purple spires, but they were not good; she
threw them into the pond.

On the surface of the pond floated small cresslike leaves of a light, bright green. Between the green patches the water was clear and dark. She squatted at the water's edge and stared down. From one corner a frog croaked, and she turned her head quickly to find him. Another frog answered. She was too late. She fixed her eyes on the spot, waiting. Frogs mate, she knew, by putting their arms around one another and squeezing. She had seen in the pond the albumenlike effluvia of their couplings. She would have liked to see that embrace. Once, when she was younger, she had stood in the dark hall upstairs, with no light but the weak night light from her room, and heard noises from her parents' room. Frightened, she had looked this way and that, not knowing what to do. What ought she do? Should she get help? She listened to their voices. Then she crept back to bed. Finally she slept, and in the morning, when she woke, late, she heard their voices again, from outside, and remembering at once, she ran to the window and saw them sitting at the far end of the garden in white garden chairs, holding their coffee cups and talking, with the sunlight fluttering over them. They were like the gods. What they broke could not be mended.

When the car turned into the driveway, Sarah did not jump up and run to greet her mother and father. Instead she lingered, poking a stick in among the reeds. But they didn't call her. Finally she went back to the house. She saw her mother's face, and then she looked at her father.

"Daddy?" she said.

He didn't answer.

"Daddy?" she repeated, touching his forearm matted with black hairs.

"What? What is it?"

"Will you play tennis with me again sometime?"

Judith looked from one to the other. "For heaven's sake," she said and ran upstairs. After a moment, they heard the shower running.

"Mommy's mad at me," said Daniel. "I made fun of Carol."

"Daddy, you shouldn't. It makes her so mad." She smiled at her father but he didn't smile back. She got out the rye bread and the cheese and two pieces of chicken and put the platter between their two places. She sat down and unfolded her paper napkin. Daniel spread mayonnaise on one slice of his bread. Carefully, he sliced the chicken and arranged the slices in neat rows, but he then moved his plate away from him and put his hands on the table where his plate had been. All he had done, he thought, was to comment that his wife's tennis partner lacked something in softness. He knew Judith thought so too, but she would never agree with him about anything any more. His strength was ebbing, his luck was sliding away from him. He buried his face in his hands. After a moment he heard Sarah leave the table and go upstairs.

In the early spring, they had gone to a marriage counselor, someone one of Judith's friends had said was "really very good." Daniel had been doubtful about the idea but Judith continued to raise the subject every few days, with a tense, distressed, absorbed expression. It rained the day they went, and they drove on the expressway out to where this woman had her office, in her house. Forsythia was blooming, and here and there were patches of dark gray snow. It was pleasant driving with Judith; for a moment he forgot where they were going. The woman's house was stucco and stone with trees around it. Her office was in the basement. He could smell the furnace. In the middle of their session, there was a knocking at the door and children's voice outside the room, calling "Mommy, Mommy, emergency." "Oh, dear," the marriage counselor had said, getting up to go to the door. "Please excuse me." When she came back, smoothing her hair and glancing at herself in the mirror, she murmured something about her housekeeper. Judith had been understanding. "After all," she said, as the woman sat down, "we are all in the same boat."

The marriage counselor implied, or so it seemed to Daniel, that they would be all right, that it was mostly a matter of sorting out priorities and resolving a few practical matters. Getting into the car afterward, he felt an immense relief. He was stirred. He wanted to kiss her. He would have liked to hold her face in his hands. As soon as he got into the car, while he was fastening his seat belt, Judith said, "How come you automatically drive?"

"Do you want to drive?" asked Daniel.

"That isn't the point," she said, with a tense chin and a shaking voice. "Why do you assume you are the driver? I can drive too, you know. It isn't the driving, it's the assuming." Daniel said that she had walked to the passenger's side, not the driver's, and so he had naturally assumed he would drive. "Yes, I know," she said bitterly. "You assumed. That's what I'm talking about." Two tears, round and brilliant, had risen in her eyes. They stood, poised and ready to fall. Daniel extended his hand to comfort her but then, fearful, withdrew it.

Judith stood in the shower with closed eyes, letting the water strike the top of her bent head. Turning, she leaned forward to feel it beat between her shoulder blades. At length, sticking one foot out, she reached for the bath mat. Out, she tucked her hair behind her ears and dried her face. She felt much better. Wiping the fogged mirror with a washcloth, she looked severely at her face, her breasts, her slender body. It was not clear to her why she had once more provoked Daniel and once more frightened Sarah, and in the mirror she saw nothing that contributed to the answer to this question. Wrapping the bath towel tightly around herself, she opened the bedroom door.

Sarah was sitting cross-legged in the middle of the bed, waiting. Her legs were scratched and crosshatched with little dots of scabs. Her knees were large, neither the knees of a grown-up nor the shadowed knees of a child. Standing in front of the dressing table, Judith observed her daughter's dogged, worried look. She sat down beside her on the edge of the bed and put her warm hand on Sarah's cool bare foot, which the child withdrew and then moved back until it touched her hand again. For several minutes they sat without speaking while Judith held her daughter's foot. They breathed in unison. Then Sarah sighed deeply and moved her foot away. She lay back on the bed.

"You're still wet, Mom," she said.

"I'll dry," said Judith. "Get your new bathing suit. I'll shorten the straps."

Sarah did not move.

"Go. Put it on."

"Now?" asked Sarah. Her cheeks were rosy, her pallor was gone. She held Judith's towel in one hand and fingered the edge. "Right now?"

At her babyish tone, Judith pulled the towel tightly around herself.

"Yes, now. Do you want to wear it before the summer is over, or not?"

In two weeks they would go back to the city. The thought of time passing confused her. Everything slid away. She herself had been a child waiting to grow up. Absorbed in thoughts of love, she had married. She had had a baby but her pregnancy had passed and she had not taken note of it, nor of Sarah's infancy, nor the days when Sarah was a little girl and had stuck out her feet to have her shoes tied. She felt she had been wheeled swiftly past the events of her life. With her friends she talked a lot about this sort of thing: marriage, liberation, fulfillment.

They talked a good deal about divorce. Carol spoke with ardor about her divorce. It was almost final; she had never been so happy, she said. For a long while she had been confused, standing still, not going anywhere, she said to Judith. And then her life began to take a direction, as it had when she was first married. Divorce was a challenge and she had been afraid of it. But now she was studying for her real-estate licensing examination. And how quickly it had all happened! It seemed unreal. "I don't want to tell you what to do," she said to Judith, just before the summer. They were at Carol's, at the loft she was sharing on White Street with a woman she had met in her real-estate class. They were eating lunch of tofu and bean sprouts. "Isn't this delicious?" said Carol, offering more to Judith. "Imagine being able to eat this way if the men were here! No, Jude. I can't tell you what to do. But I can say that the main thing for you to do is to become aware of your needs." Her therapist had helped make it clear to her that the husband you choose when your expectations are based on old values will naturally become intolerable to you when you are aware of your needs. Carol was doing yoga. She said it made her aware of things she never dreamed of. She urged Judith to try it.

In the evenings, when Daniel came home and asked about her day, Judith often did not say she had had lunch with Carol. But, in a way, concealment was not something new. As a child, she had learned to be watchful. Playing, she tiptoed about, listening for her mother, who wore clothing that made a whispering sound. Judith could tell, always, when her mother was coming. It was essential, she believed, to be on guard at all times lest the adults take note of what she was doing. For they, being adults, would take away the little object she had picked up from her father's desk, her mother's dressing table. They would unfold her closed fingers or pinch her cheeks to make her spit out what it was she had in her mouth. Holding her between their knees, they would insert their finger into her mouth and sweep it from corner to corner to extract every last bit. She felt the big ridges of the skin of their finger against her tongue. She could have bit. But she did not. Instead, she let her lips go slack. She looked up at them while they cleaned out her mouth. Weakly, she smiled, agreeing that she was a foolish little girl to have put the blue marble or the candy or the smooth mothball into her mouth, foolish to want the things she shouldn't want, whether she had wanted them greedily as the candy or experimentally as the mothball. She had been foolish to be so desirous, and now she was on their side, almost cleaning out her own mouth, Mommy's little silly now become Mommy's big girl who spits it all into Mommy's hand.

"OK. Here I am. In this thing." Sarah stood before her mother with a pleased expression in her new bathing suit. She posed with her arms in the air, turning slowly. The large bones of her pelvis showed through her scanty flesh. Her navel was shallow. The fold of the bottom half of her suit covered her neatly. Above, her breasts were small.

"Do you like it?"

"I like it a lot," said Judith. She opened her legs and the ends of the towel fell between them. She pointed to the floor to show where she wanted her to stand, and when the child was facing her Judith leaned forward and quickly kissed her on the smooth brown skin between the two halves of her bathing suit.

Sarah objected. "Oh, Mother," she said.

"I couldn't help it," Judith said. "Now hold still," she said, closing her knees around her daughter, as she tried to tighten the little straps that laced the sides, but one strap was too short and slipped out of its knot. "Sarah," she said, "don't wiggle."

Sarah was trying to look over her shoulder to see herself in the mirror.

"Sarah!" Judith gripped her daughter between her knees, but the child, outraged, tore herself away.

"Mother!" She glared at Judith. "You hurt me." She backed away and stood against the wall in the dark red bikini with the little strings hanging loose at her sides. The brassiere of the suit was twisted, and one breast was uncovered. Her little breast was pale all but at the center, where the nipple softly bulged. Sarah looked down and pulled the fabric over her breast. To her mother she said she thought the bathing suit was stupid and stalked out of the room. But Judith heard her slow steps change, as soon as she reached the stairs, to a rush. Then the screen door banged as she went out.

On the porch, the black kitten was crossing from the sofa, where he had been batting a loose piece of wicker, to the garden, when Sarah intercepted him. She picked him up and held him against her stomach, stroking his faintly damp fur. Raising him to the level of her face, she looked into his tan eyes. Then she sat down on the sofa and ran two fingers on either side of the light little bones of his spine.

From his body an animal warmth began to spread. A sigh broke the regularity of his shallow breaths. He began to tremble and quiver. Sarah stroked his back, first downward, in the direction his fur grew, and then the other way. At once, his eyes flared open and he fanned his whiskers. Sarah tightened her grip and said, "Now, kitty, there's a good kitty," in a threatening voice, but the little cat stiffened and lowered his head to squeeze out of her hands. Sarah tried to hold on to him, at the same time avoiding his claws, while maintaining all the while that she was patting the kitten whom she loved and who loved her, but he arched and pulled himself out of her hands and disappeared under the porch. Sarah brought the scratch on her forearm to her lips and licked the blood away.

On the other hand, thought Daniel, who had finished his sandwich, it is perfectly possible that there is no hope at all. He put his plate and glass into the sink. It was the first time he had spoken, albeit silently, these words, and

they were followed by a chill that suffused his entire body.
Quickly, he went to the foot of the stairs down which
Sarah was rushing. He had to step aside to let her pass.
She hurried by him and out the front door. He scarcely
saw her. He started to climb the stairs with his head bent,
absorbed in the dull, strange sensations that this thought
had loosed in him. At the landing he stopped and stood
still. In the landing window were two panes of colored
glass, one violet and one blue, and while he continued to
ponder, he squinted at the vegetable garden, first through
one, then the other, enjoying, in a mechanical way, the
intensity of the color and registering the fact that the colored glass, even at such a painful moment, had retained
its power to turn the rows of plants first violet, then blue.
Why should it be true, he thought, that although everyone
knows that nothing lasts, I should insist that it does? His
thoughts then proceeded in an orderly way, as though
along an already prepared track. He saw, as though on a
television screen, a woman's head with disheveled hair
followed by a succession of human heads with open mouths.

"Dan? Is that you?"

His wife appeared in the doorway of the bedroom, wearing white pants and a white shirt. Her hair, still wet, touched
her cheeks in dark points. She was carefully rolling up her
sleeves.

"I think I really hurt her feelings," she said. "Damn."

Daniel stared at her. He could not tell whether she looked
young or old. He climbed the remaining stairs and stood
at the bedroom door.

"I'm going for corn," she said. "It's his last night."

"Yes," he said. "I know."

As she passed, she touched him lightly on the arm. "I'll
be back in a little while," she said, but Daniel reached for
her hand and held it, looking down at her arm, her hand,
her damp curly hair.

"Oh," she said. "Well, maybe you should take your
shower first."

133

Later, as she was backing out of the garage to get the corn, Judith looked into the rearview mirror and saw her father walking up the driveway, back from the beach. Leaving the ignition on, she waited until he reached her and stood beside the car. He put his hand through the open window and rested it on her arm. His hand was hot. He was trailing a beach towel and holding a newspaper under his arm.

"Where are you going?" he asked. "I'll go with you."

"You got sunburned," she said.

"Yes," he said. "I stayed out too long." He touched her cheek.

Judith hesitated. What could she say to him as they drove?

"I'll be right back," she said.

As soon as she reached the highway she accelerated. The pavement glittered. She was glad she had her sunglasses. Turning up the radio, she drove west, with the sun big and white, even through her dark glasses, hanging right over the middle of the road.

At the farm stand, she had picked eight ears of corn and was waiting to pay for them when she saw a fresh supply of corn arriving. The farmer's wife was guiding the new ears as they tumbled from the burlap bag her son held over the table. Judith put her corn down and stood close to the table, waiting to choose the best ones.

At sunset the breeze, which had died down, began to blow again, fitfully. Just to be safe, Daniel set the grill in the shelter of a corner of the house. Even so, as soon as he started the fire, the flames leaned to the side and burned fiercely with a roaring sound. When they had subsided and the coals were white, he stood beside the grill with his head bent and the tongs in one hand, watching, as the fresh fat sputtered, to see that the meat was seared but not blackened, careful to turn each piece without piercing it lest the juices escape and drip into the fire. The whole task pleased him from the beginning to the moment he would set the platter on the porch table and Judith come rushing from the kitchen with the corn.

It was not clear to him now what he felt, or what he thought he could expect.

Saul, leaving Sarah to put the husks in the garbage, was walking across the lawn to stand next to him while he finished the steaks.

It was nearly dark.

"Ready, Daddy? Mommy says call when you are ready."

Saul put his hand on Daniel's shoulder. He had no part to play, Daniel thought, either in the cooking of the corn or in broiling the meat.

Having checked the thickest piece, Daniel turned toward the house and called, "It's time!"

"Daddy says 'time,' Mommy! Daddy says 'time!'"

"All right, I hear you," called Judith, from inside. "They're in."

Sarah came leaping across the lawn. "The sparks, the sparks!" she cried. "They're going up like fireflies."

Saul warned her about getting too close to the fire.

"One more minute," murmured Daniel, poised over the grill. Saul held the platter close to the fire.

From the house, Judith called Sarah to come get the salad.

"Ready!" called Judith. "Here I come!" Holding the bowl in two hands, she kicked open the screen door. In the bright light from the kitchen, Daniel saw she was trying to keep her face turned away from the steam rising from the pale corn.

"OK," said Daniel, holding the platter carefully as he stepped up onto the porch with Saul behind him. "Here it is!"

"We're eating really late," said Sarah, when they were sitting down. "Aren't we eating late, Daddy?"

In their glass cylinders, the two candles ducked and jumped. The wind was blowing in the tops of the trees, and from their restless, bending branches came a rushing sound like the sound of the sea. Across the sky, clouds moved rapidly in formations lit by the moon, which appeared and disappeared as they drew together and apart. Every now and then the wind ceased, and for a moment the roar of the surf could be heard and the groan of receding waves.

Sarah looked up from her plate. "It sounds rough," she said, "doesn't it?"

"Children," began Saul, but the wind rose and they had to lean forward to hear him.

"What, Daddy? What did you say?" Judith turned to her father.

"Nothing," he said, after a pause. "I just wanted to thank you for such a nice week."

"Oh, Daddy, please," said Judith.

With her book open beside her, Sarah was lying on her side, in bed. All during the end of dinner, as they were drinking their coffee, and after, while she put the dishes into the dishwasher and Saul scrubbed the corn pot, she had been thinking about going back to her book, but when she had said good night, and gone upstairs, she could not find her place. She turned the pages back and forth, and although she skimmed passages she knew she had read she could not be sure exactly where she had stopped. She decided to go back and read the part about the ball all over again, but even though she found she still could make herself feel like Kitty, excited and pretty in her gown, after several pages she raised her head and said, not quite out loud, but nearly, "I think this book is too old for me." After a while she turned off the light and put her head down on the pillow. She lay in the dark, hearing the wind and the waves and watching the fast-moving shadows of the branches on the wall of her room.

When Judith came upstairs to go to bed, she saw two

slits of light in the hall. Both Saul and Sarah were still awake. Later, she opened the bedroom door and saw that only her father's light was on. She opened Sarah's door.

"It's me," she whispered into the dark room.

"I know it's you," said the child somewhat irritably. "I always know when it's you."

Judith sat on the edge of the bed. The moon came out from behind the clouds.

"It's light as day," said the mother.

"Oh, Mother," said Sarah, "you always exaggerate."

Judith leaned over the bed to smooth the blanket. She felt the book lying on the bed and placed it on the night table. "How's the book?" she asked.

"OK," said the child. But in the middle of her mother's kiss, she tightened her thin arms around Judith's neck and held on so tightly Judith had to shake herself free.

"Good night, Mom," said Sarah, lying back.

Under his door, Saul's light gleamed. Judith took a step toward her father's room. Beside her, on the moonlit wall, black shadows of leaves stirred. The spindles of the banister shone white in the moonlight. Downstairs, in the hall, small squares of light lay on the floor as the power of the moon pressed into the house. Outside, the trees shifted in the cool air. The breeze shivered and the tops of the hedges shook pollen and sweetness into the air. The odor of the blooming hedges rose through the house. Judith was suffused with power. She felt the moon like something expanding in her chest, as if it might burst at any moment. She extended her hand to her father's door.

She knocked softly, saying "Daddy?" and pressed the door open.

He lay on the bed, leaning upon a stiff pillow that was propped against the wall behind him. In the yellow light from the reading lamp his closed eyes were in deep shadow. They looked like the hollows of the eyes of a blind man. In sleep, his features drooped and his mouth lay slackly open. Thwarted and in confusion, Judith wanted to be out of the room. She slid the book out from under his heavy hand and carefully preserved his place. She was anxious to avoid the sleeping man, but before she turned out the light, while she was reaching under the lampshade for the chain, he opened his eyes. His expression changed in no way. He gave no acknowledgment of her presence, he merely made a very soft noise, a soft grunt, and closed his eyes again.

Fears

꩜ ꩜ On the day the president of Egypt was assassinated, Jim Pettit's little boy had stayed home from school with a temperature. In the middle of the morning, his mother found him sitting on the floor of the living room looking at television.

"Let me tie your bathrobe," she said. "It's too chilly to be sitting there with your bathrobe open."

He didn't look around. When she glanced at the screen to see what he was watching, she knew by the chaotic way the camera was moving that again something bad had happened.

A while later Jim telephoned from his office in Greenfield. He had heard the news on the car radio, but he hadn't called her right away, he said, because he hoped it wasn't true.

"It's true," she said.

"I know it's true," said Jim.

She said she thought Robert might not have understood what he had seen. He could have thought he was looking at a movie, she said.

"Perhaps," said Jim.

In the evening, the children made brownies with their mother while Jim watched the news, turning from channel to channel. Then he went outside and breathed the cold night air.

The next day Robert was well, and the following day he went back to school.

On Friday, Jim drove the five miles home from work as the sun set and the sky flamed. Yellow stacks of freshly split wood sat beside each house, and in the opening of sheds and outbuildings he could see the same raw color. An occasional meadow was still bright green, and here and there a dark horse raised its head as he drove by. Remembering they were to use the car later, he left it halfway out of the shed, where his own firewood was stacked. His wife was in the kitchen, straightening up after the children's supper. He kissed her on the cheek. She put down the sponge and turned to him for another kiss.

"Make your drink," she said. "I have a few more things to do."

The children were waiting for him in the living room. Robert was in his dinosaur pajamas, and the younger child, Lizzie, wore a thick one-piece suit with padded feet. An outsized zipper ran up to her chin.

Jim put his drink down on the coffee table and took off his glasses to receive their embraces.

When they were all sitting on the rug near the fire, he put his glasses back on. Lizzie moved into his lap. "Daddy," she said and pressed his cheek with her hand. She stroked his sleeve, touched the buttons of his jacket, patted his face. She was rosy from her bath and her fingers smelled of soap. He took her wandering hand and held it still.

"Daddy!" she said.

Releasing her hand, he ran his finger over her fine pale hair. She looked up at him with a fierce expression.

"Tell us a story," she said. "Tell."

Robert, who was six, sat with his legs straight out in front of him. He rotated his feet in their new bedroom slippers and watched the elastic stretch and retract. His eyes were brown and his hair was smooth and brown. Where his sister was fat and flushed, he was thin. He was sitting slightly apart from his father and sister, and although he kept his eyes on his slippers, having noticed that the firelight lent them a shine which could be made to slide from the toe to the heel by twisting his foot, every now and then he directed a quick look at his father. He busied himself with slippers, dinosaurs, and whatever diversions the fire could offer: sparks, gleams, the collapse of a burnt-out log, but when he looked up his glance measured the distance between his father and his sister. He waited.

"All right, kitty cats," said Jim. "What shall it be?"

"Ticky tats," said the little girl.

"Kitty cats," said Robert. "Kitty cats." He was mocking his father, who would not have said "kitty cats" had he been directing his attention only at him. His father could make him laugh when he didn't want to, and often did, by saying things like "kitty cats" and worse.

Suddenly he felt tired of keeping this stiff watch and unbending guard. He sighed, acknowledging a kind of defeat, and moved in closer to Daddy and Lizzie.

"All right," said Jim. "Ready?"

Lizzie put her thumb in her mouth and then took it out and looked at it. It was wet. "Ready," she said.

Jim began the story: "Once there was a little girl and her name was Missy. She was a very good little girl. She always did whatever her mother asked her to do, and she always did what her father asked her to do. In nursery school she was good, and she was good in the supermarket. She stayed on her side in the car and she never forgot to brush her hair. She smiled at the good and frowned at the bad—"

"And sometimes she was very sad," said Robert, rapidly and in a slightly confused tone as though surprised to find himself saying anything at all.

"No," said his father. "She wasn't actually ever sad. She was quite happy. Reasonably happy."

Both children looked at him. The little boy moved closer and the father reached toward him and grasped with two fingers of one hand the slender column of the back of his neck. The child put his head to one side to relish the feeling and to bear the happiness that had begun to mount inside him. He let his eyes close.

The little girl shifted her weight on Jim's thigh, and he, feeling a sudden strain in his back, said, "Why are we sitting on the floor? Let's go sit on the couch."

They stood up.

From the couch the fire looked far away and formal.

"Daddy!" said the little girl imperiously.

He put an arm around each of them and started again: "But one fine day—"

"Jim, not too scary." His wife had stopped in the doorway to look at them. Her arms were full of bath towels. Later, when the children were in bed, they would have a quick supper, and then, as they sometimes did on Friday evening, as soon as the neighbor's daughter came they would drive down to Greenfield and go to the movies.

"And then?" said Robert.

Lizzie was standing up on Jim's leg. He could feel her toes inside her rubberized pajama soles as she tried to balance on his thigh. Gently, by pressing his hand against the small of her back, he persuaded her to sit down. "But one day, one fine and cloudless day, when Missy had gone with her nursery school class to buy fish food for the class goldfish, she got separated from the other children and the teacher, and she found herself all alone in the middle of the shopping center. She looked down the arcade on her right and saw no one. Then she looked to the left and saw no one there. She was all alone." The story went on, almost by itself. He knew he wasn't doing his best. Sometimes his stories amazed him. Some stories poured through him as though they came from somewhere else; they bemused even the teller, and he could imagine that years from now, when the children were grown up, they would remember the best ones, like the Boy Who Had X-ray Vision, or the one about the children who lived in the woods on the far side of the dump.

He went on, speaking in a soft voice, and told them how Missy was at last rescued from the locked and echoing supermarket by a certain first-grade boy whose intelligence in deducing her location was equaled only by his agility in squeezing into narrow places. "And so the boy, having found his way into the warehouse, edged past boxes and cartons and crates. How dark it was! He knew, however, that he must not let himself be frightened. If he panicked, he would not be able to tell which cartons held paper towels and paper diapers and toilet paper—the large light ones that rocked if you gave them a little push—and which, heavier and pungent, held soap powder and soap flakes. For then he'd never find Missy, whose voice he had heard over the intercom before the power failed, telling him she was between the dog food and the place where the candy was. 'Courage,' he said to himself, and so, listening and feeling and sniffing, he made his way."

Jim glanced from his son to his daughter and saw by their grave, wide-opened eyes and their parted lips that their hearts lay with the lost girl and the brave frightened boy. His own heart went out to them and he decided, while he was speaking, to edit one or two effects he had had in mind and hasten the dénouement.

The fire made a popping noise.

The children were sitting close to their father. Robert was holding one of his father's hands in his hands.

As he finished the story, Jim could hear the children breathing.

"And then she went home?" asked his daughter.

"And then she went home," he said.

The movie took place in California. The camera slid around a house in such a way as to induce apprehension in the viewer. In the house lived one of the main characters, a fifty-year-old woman, played by an actress who was making a movie for the first time in many years. Jim was reminded of his youth by the sight of her face. He had liked her in college and even in high school. There was a lot of driving in the movie, particularly by women, who got in and out of their cars in a way characteristic of women in movies and on television. The way they slammed car doors and drove away said: This is California, this is modern life, this is dangerous and exciting. The woman lived alone in the house, and in the evening, after her housekeeper and gardener went home, it was clear she was in danger. She had lovers. Someone was going to kill her. One of her lovers was going to kill her. Her death was prolonged. Jim knew at some point his wife would turn her head away. When she did, he smiled and gave her a little pat.

"Tell me when it's over," she said.

"It's only ketchup," he said.

"I don't think so," she whispered back.

During the time the several police officers were weighing the probable involvement of the known suspects, the minor characters were portrayed in places familiar to non-Californians from other movies: at a Pacific beach house, at an orange ranch, and at a dusty gas station and general store at a crossroads in the desert. The killer did turn out to be one of her lovers, but not the obvious one. The shootout took place at the tiny motel where the housekeeper's aged mother lived.

"How did you like it?" asked Jim in the lobby, feeling for the car keys.

"Horrible," said his wife. "They said he was an American Lelouch. I'm sorry I brought you."

"You didn't make me come," he said. "Anyway, I liked it."

They drove home through the quiet countryside. From time to time their headlights picked out of the darkness a tree whose leaves had turned yellow or flashed on the black windowpanes of a farmhouse where everyone had gone to bed. "I think we could use some heat," said Jim, and turned the knob for the heater and the one for the fan. After a minute they felt the warm air. It was soothing to drive through the pale autumn fields. Neither spoke. Just before the road started its rise toward their village, it passed through a marshy place where mist was thick on either side and they were plunged into milky obscurity. Jim reached with his right hand under his wife's skirt and felt for the elasticized edge of her underpants.

At home, she paid the baby-sitter and watched at the window while the girl ran across the road to her own house, where the outside light was on. When the light went off, she let the curtain drop and went upstairs. She pushed the children's door open over the stiff new carpet, and Jim stood in the doorway while she touched both children and adjusted the window and the shade. Then they went together into their own room.

Much later in the night, he woke up. The television was still on. Dread had seized him in his sleep. He had dreamed they were all in a train, his wife and both children, and the outside of the train was being pounded by bullets. There was a terrible racket of metal against metal, and it was not at all clear he was going to be able to continue to protect them. Awake, he was as afraid as he had been asleep. He lay still and waited for his arms and legs to stop trembling.

After a while he felt calmer. He turned on his side, toward the television. It was a movie, in black and white, set in Prague during World War II, about three Czech exiles who parachuted into Czechoslovakia on a mission to kill the Reichskommissar; one of the three, it seemed, had betrayed the others. Intrigued now, and wide awake, he reached for his wife's extra pillow, which was lying between them, and stuck it under his head. His heart was still beating heavily. The room was silvery. He stretched his legs and began to relax. The wife, or the girlfriend, of one of the exiles came and went, bringing messages. There was a lot of running. It must have been the sound of gunfire from the television he had heard in his dream. In the dream he had tried to lie on top of the children to protect them from bullets. He had tried to lie on top of them without hurting them.

In the crypt of St. Vitus, the two loyal Czechs met their heroic end while gunfire sounded from the street.

When the movie was over, he turned to the news channel and watched a summary of the events of the week. The film had been edited. He was never able to find what his wife said Robert had seen: the arm, the clothing, the expression on the injured man's face.

He saw the sky above Cairo and the plumes of colored smoke expanding as the formation of Mirages flew by the reviewing stand. Within the reviewing stand the chairs were all turned over. It looked as though no one was there, but then, like anemones on the sea floor, the chairs started to move and wave about, and one by one the men appeared from beneath the chairs, their hands first, as they reached from below for leverage to help them rise.

Meditation
on Play,
Thoughts
on Death

〜 〜

For years, my son Jacob, who is now twelve, played so hard at dramas of such complexity that when the episode was over he would emerge from his room damp-skinned and spent. He and Astrid, friends since they were four, used to plan these afternoons. As they grew older, they would sometimes speak on the telephone: "You bring all your G.I. Joe stuff to my house." Separately they would collect equipment they could see they together might need. Heavy pieces of furniture would be moved by these two small strong children, beds and desks fitted together at right angles, over which they fastened the bedspreads and blankets dragged from beds. Mommy, can we use this? Can we take these? The door to the linen closet would be left ajar, the light slanting across the hall; a trail of disturbed washcloths, pillowcases, and pillow feathers led to Jacob's room, where the shades would be drawn and the doors closed. Behind these closed doors they constructed flight decks of carriers and the cockpits of fighter planes to attack enemies entrenched upon Pacific islands in caves of impregnable rock. The skies swarmed, the seas heaved. Glittering metal hung overhead and fell spinning into the ocean, upon which, in their tiny craft, Jacob and Astrid slipped between menacing hulls to safety and revenge. From his room emerged murmurs of strategy and shouts of pain, exhortations to courage and wild cries to persuade a lurking spy that forces were on the point of landing on the beaches below. But in fact the children were cut off, threatened by enemies on both sides. The jungles were alive with snipers, unseen rapids roared, beneath leafy camouflage gun muzzles gleamed. One could only hold one's breath, the challenge was so great. A long silent moment of fear acknowledged the extent of the danger. Perhaps there was no hope at all. And then from somewhere unexpected, perhaps through an unnoticed break in the glowering sky, deliverance stood at hand. And all those circling enemies were undone. No one expected so quick a solution. It seemed that the game could have gone on and on. But the moment of utmost strain had borne its own release, and all gave way in one triumphant rush.

Thereupon they would call, "Come. Come. See what we have made," and I would push open the door and in the room, which was now orange with late-afternoon light, I could smell the sweat of their excitement. "We're in here." Turning back a blanket corner, I saw that there they were together in the back of some cavern in warm darkness. I saw their eyes and their glistening skin. Astrid would sometimes look a bit shy and self-mocking as the shades snapped up and bright winter light fell upon their works, but never Jacob, who would explain with pride that here had lain the console, there the radar screen, that between this point and that electronically sensitive cells—and here he would point to a little row of worn batteries, or perhaps cans of tomato paste—had transmitted to the space station the locations of those whom they had just now overcome. Sometimes they would look over the battlegrounds and sigh. It was clearly all over. And then they would leave the wreckage and the tumbled sheets and rush to the kitchen to eat big bowls of sweet things and stir up sticky milk drinks.

Well, of course I am telescoping how many afternoons? Many. And as for us with sex, or dinner parties, one time is not always as good as another, so from time to time inspiration failed them. Then Jacob might find that, without knowing how, he had pinched Astrid, or punched her, and she would become silent and her clear face darken and they would have to resort to television and wait until it was time for the visit to be over. But the next time could be the best. Some freshly conceived invention would spring up to urge the two children to valorous acts they had not known even in their dreams; new contraptions of war would push open Jacob's door and proliferate the length of the hall, newly shaped, like Themistocles's wall, of building blocks torn from the ramparts of older fortifications, bastions against an earlier enemy. The convention of privacy was abandoned as the theater of war swept from room to room. They didn't care if I saw them. They didn't care who saw them. They were airborne.

Sometimes, during the week, in preparation, Jacob made armor, weapons ancient or modern, electronic weaponry, or perhaps a crossbow, or simply arrows. But just as often the machinery of war was born in the field, it flew together in Jacob's hand as the need arose. As when some great warrior found his sword struck from his hand, and he stood stockstill, helpless, watching the blade of his mortal enemy gleam ominously while he could still see the two pieces of his own blade, split and lying in the grass, and then, as though by a miracle, a new spear twinkled in his hand, so for these children the speed with which their ordnance was delivered was sometimes dazzling.

Now Astrid was endangered, shipwrecked. Firepower poured from the heavens, thunder rose from the depths of the sea. How could he reach her, with their landing craft hopelessly crippled, great lacy holes blown out of her sides, and the stretch of water between them menacing the sky in angry leaps? But always resourceful, he shouted across to her and strode to the grove of trees on the finger of land at the end of his island and chopped them down, trimmed the branches, split them into boards, and planed them smooth; next he pegged them together and fitted a mast and a rudder. Astrid leaned over from her island to hand him a sheet. "Here, this is for a sail," she said and then stepped back in the shelter of the overhanging cliff. Now the craft was ready. Watchfully he slid her in between the

waves and with cunning steered her from trough to trough.
So skillful was he that not a drop of water touched his
skin, his mast stood unbroken, his sail stretched untorn.
The raft flew between the crests of the waves, sending up
a spray of foam on each side. A single sea bird skimmed
alongside whose wings sometimes touched the surface, and
then little spurts of water jetted up on either side of him
too. Jacob stood straight and proud, one arm wrapped
around the mast, a frown of concentration upon his brow,
his eyes sternly alert for trouble. And trouble there was,
for a wave rose which confounded all his cunning and lifted
the raft as though it were no heavier than a leaf. It lifted
raft and rider into the sky and separated one from the other.
They spun apart and twisted in the roaring air until the
wind dropped for a moment and they fell like two gannets
into the sea. Astrid stood up and tried to guide the swim-
mer through the storm. "Here, here," she shouted over
the shrieking wind and thumping surf as he tried to raise
his head above the waves to find a place on shore where
he could drag himself out and not be crushed against the
rocks. But salt stung his eyes and green waves hid the land.
Splinters of his little craft appeared and disappeared in the
heaving sea. "Here, here," cried Astrid in alarm and crawled
on hands and knees as far as she dared on the treacherous
rocks to reach out a hand to Jacob, whom she slowly and
with many a near mishap pulled out of the water. He lay
on the ground and gasped for breath. She saw his briny
hair, his wild eyes, and his stern mouth. "It could have
been terrible," she said. "You could have drowned."

Or it could be night. Jacob and Astrid, spies, dressed in
black, were creeping through the damp woods, past black
tree trunks and gleaming wreckage of airplanes, past the
blasted frame of a small tank here, there its cover sunk into
the soft wet leaves, and everywhere fallen comrades. But
no time now to dwell upon grief, to linger in sorrow. Time
now only to look sharp, to know the dark like the animals,
to turn to any sound a wolf's ear, to see with the staring

eyes of the cat. Silence. Silence and cunning. One must not even whisper. In the zone of silence only gestures are permitted.

Scouting ahead, where the trees broke and the marsh began, Jacob peered with watchful slits of eyes into the dark line of swamp grasses. He saw nothing, but he knew that the creatures of the marsh were watching him. Tense herons blinked and ducks paddled out from the reeds. Angry swans stretched forward their long necks. The night world was uneasy, as he was, waiting. Something was about to happen. What was it? He looked back to see Astrid pointing straight up and with her other arm waving him back to her. For an instant he hesitated, uncertain whether or not to relinquish to her his accustomed managerial prerogative, for his own drama had not quite crystallized, but she was waving insistently and so he returned to her side and looked up to see traces of pale flares tumble from star to star in the night sky and fade into weak lines. These faltering lines marked the east and the west, the north and the south, all the starry quarters of the night, but in the center of the sky, spreading over the moon and her pulsing light, little bursts of darkness puffed noiselessly. Almost immediately it was completely dark, but both children knew that slowly descending upon them were the hundreds and hundreds of parachutes of the enemy.

Plans formed in their minds. Their thoughts raced. The lure of danger, the thrill of the battle to come, pride in their skill, in their loyalty, stirred them. Now they were in for it. This was the real thing. What to do? To flee? To hide? But that's not what they were here for.

In the silence, as the parachutists floated toward them, there sounded all at once a terrible squeal and then silence again and then the cry of the heron, and the flapping of heavy wings, and cries of birds together and separately, the brassy sounds of outrage and distress. Against all that racket the vow of military silence no longer needed to be observed, and the children drew close to one another in the shelter of a great oak tree. Are we to die now? they asked one another. Here? At the edge of the great swamp where our bodies will fall to be nibbled by the fishes and nipped by crocodiles? Is this the end of it all? Is this the meaning of all our struggles, all the times we thought of a plan, all the mazes we found our way out of, the ambushes we outflanked, the tricks we outschemed? Has all our valor and wit only brought us to this dreadful end? Better to have gone down with our companions in a hail of bullets, holding upright our country's flag with our last ounce of strength, than be strangled silently here in the dark by some parachutist whose face we cannot see even if only to mock him in his triumph. Astrid took Jacob's two hands in hers and they looked long and hard at one another, for they could now see despite the extreme darkness. From the sky above they heard the creaking of harnesses and the straining of cloth. Now they were in for it. Now it was up to them. This was the moment they had trained themselves for, the test they had come all this way to meet. They had not known what form it would take, whether their trial would be by water or fire, by night or day, whether they would confront it armed or empty-handed, but they were confident that once they set out, comradely and with stout hearts, sooner or later their chance would come. Suddenly, when you aren't looking up, it comes out of the sky; when you are squinting at the far mountains, the first ships of the armada creep over the horizon behind your back, and when you turn around and see them, your heart pounds and your hands get cold, but what happens then is up to you.

One time, Astrid was wounded. There was no blood to be seen, but they both had heard something crack. The vast polar outreaches stretched away in all directions. Freezing wind drove the snow in slanting lines between their anxious faces. Astrid fell back against the snowbank. Her face was pale and she kept her eyes fixed upon Jacob's face. "I think I'm wounded really badly," she gasped. "I

don't think I can go on. Maybe you should leave me here."
The white snow was grayer now and was falling faster and
more thickly. The wind screamed and the dogs muttered
and circled around the sleds, eager to speed on. There was
snow on their snouts. It was clear that the cold and the
snow excited them. They snorted and sneezed and shook
their heads to get the snow off their ears. They pulled at
their leashes and padded as far as their harness would let
them toward the great white distance. The line between
sky and land was blotted away. The glittering cascades of
ice, which only moments ago had offered promise of shelter and threat of ambush, were gone. Only snow. Soft dull
snow everywhere. And wind. And cold. Jacob knew that
one should never lie down in the snow. He knew that he
could not leave Astrid in the snow. He knew that that way
lay death. She would freeze to death in the snow. Lying
under the cutting wind, how long could she last? All their
ammunition was on the dogsled. It would have to go. The
dogs could not pull the sled burdened with Astrid and the
rifles both. It was too much. The guns would have to be
unloaded. He could come back for them later, when he
had got her to a doctor. Astrid was watching him with
troubled eyes. "I'm sorry," she murmured. "Leave me. I'll
be all right." Impossible, he thought, seeing her there,
trying to drag herself onto her good side. With furious
sudden energy flowing in his body, he lifted the heavy
oblong ammunition boxes from the sled and set them neatly
down in the snow. He took off his fur-lined parka and
spread it fur side up on the sled, and with strength and
power sent to him by the great goddess he bent and lifted
his wounded comrade and gently laid her, whose anxious
eyes had never left his face, upon the furry couch. She
never once moaned even when he had to move her dangling leg, but when she was at last stretched out on the
sled, she shuddered with relief at being so still and being
able to take her eyes away from him and just look up at
the cottony snow as he trotted back and forth, straight-

ening the harness lines and speaking quickly in a low tone to the dogs, clearing the blades of the runners of thick dirty clogs of ice, and laying the reins out straight in a semicircle like the ribs of a fan. Then he came back to her and put the reins into her hands in a bunch; the leather was dark from the sweat of his hands. Now the dogs were snuffing and whimpering. Each one stood in his place. Jacob brushed from the sled the snow that had fallen on it while he had been working. He brushed away the snow that had fallen upon Astrid's body and hair, and then he climbed onto the sled and drew over them both the rugs of animal skins that were piled at their feet, fur rugs of lynx and seal and polar bear, and then he too lay back. Side by side the children lay together in the sleigh gazing up at the sky, which was dark and white at the same time. Muffled by the falling snow so that it seemed more an echo than a call, they heard the resonant cry of the snow goose and then directly over-head the rumble of the wing beats of the heavy birds. Unseen they passed overhead, beating their way through the snowy night. It would snow for ever and ever. Astrid gave the reins a smart snap and the dogs howled with joy and with one concerted effort dislodged the sled from its icy mooring. The children could feel the jerks and tugs of their starting up through their heels and the backs of their legs, their buttocks and shoulder blades, and through the backs of their skulls. It was dizzying to lie there so still, not even seeing the dogs, only the sky, while every bump and pull was received in their bodies.

Finally they each felt at the same moment the great smoothing out of it all as the dogs increased their speed and the jerks and skids evened out into trembles and a smooth swinging as the ecstatic dogs made their way over the icy crust faster and faster until it seemed to the children lying there with their eyes staring straight up that they had left the land entirely and were rising to meet the snow and the vague pale colors that pulsed dimly everywhere in the sky.

All right. For seven or eight years they played together in this fashion. It seemed remarkable to me. Not the fact that they played at war and danger—after all, that in itself is usual for children—but the profusion of their inventions bespoke powers that awed me. Who would not have envied them? And when the play was done and all those towering constructions became merely chairs piled on tables, with what delicious ease did they abandon the field to loll about languorously in the kitchen eating cookies and laughing.

As I said, Jacob now is twelve. He studies Latin and struggles with the violin. He has immense black hockey skates. At night he wears something to bed called a night arch to urge back his front teeth. Astrid has braces and breasts and has gown as tall as a small woman. One day, recently, Jacob said to me, "I remember Astrid's teeth when she was little. They were so tiny and cute." At once I could see those minute brilliant white points in her beautiful mouth, spaced with an architectural perfection, quite far apart, each one placed just so on the ridge of her gum. I was struck that he could remember how she looked so long ago. I had thought that for a child the world is changeless. I wouldn't have thought that children notice one another grow any more than a child notices himself growing. With no sense of change there could be no place for nostalgia to flourish. But I look about and see change in every quarter. In the strange film on the dog's eye and in the cracked bindings of books I think of as new, just bought, as well as in the cracks and films on faces I see across the room or in the mirror. What I mean is that I am growing old, and I cannot forget it for a minute. But when Jacob spoke with nostalgia for Astrid's long-gone little teeth I was distressed and wanted to stand between him and such thoughts. I wanted to stop up those cracks that can at any moment widen into great rifts through which I can see the shifting sands below. At the same time I wanted to conceal my distress, as though there was something unseemly about it. It's one thing to smile and wave as the plane taxis to the far runway; fears can be dissimulated to some degree, anxieties can be masked. But I want to conceal from my son what even Thetis could not conceal from hers: what Jacob seems already to know. Because yesterday after he had walked Astrid to the bus stop and waited with her in the steely blue afternoon, Jacob stood at my study door with cheeks glorious and eyes a bit red-rimmed from the cold. Despite his raging cheeks he looked serious, even a bit burdened. I turned off my typewriter. "It was no good. It was no good last time either," he said.

He came in and sat opposite me, frowning and determined, with the faintest overlay of the theatrical, which in no way detracted from the gravity his face and voice bore. He said he couldn't play any more; not only could he not play with Astrid, he couldn't even play with boats in the bathtub. He said he had gotten to be like everyone else who could only play games that come in boxes, games with spinners. Spinners and pieces you move about on a board. He said he was getting to be like all the children he knew who were always collecting things. That's all they wanted to do, collect things like stamps or rocks, and sort them and put them in boxes, or things like baseball cards and keep them in bundles with thick rubber bands around their middles, or things like matchbooks or comic books or bottle caps or coins. Then they trade these with one another, or they go to the stamp store or the coin store or the comic book store and buy more. He said that last year he and Astrid had noticed that the game was all talking and let's do this and you be that, and it had no action, that somehow just before they were going to get up from their planning and props to really play, when the fortifications were all in place and the guns ready and the radar screens twisting, something would happen to them and they just couldn't start. They could only talk. And he had thought it was all over. But then there had been some sort of a reprieve, a remission, and for a year they had played more brilliantly, more feverishly, than ever. Tundras had been vaster with snowstorms more blinding, enemies more cunning; the children themselves had fashioned more dashing uniforms and had extricated themselves from more desperate situations than they earlier ever had imagined. But now it was no good. And it wouldn't be again. He knew that. His voice suddenly thickened and his eyes showed tears. It's sad, he said.

Next he said that he could remember when he was little and happy. What do you remember? I asked, and he answered, Running on the campus at night. I pictured him when he was four, with red, red cheeks, in the winter, with his nose running a little bit, and it growing dark with the lights coming on on the campus walks, maybe the Christmas lights are on here and there, and a few stars and a weak moon, and along the paths from building to building, between the monuments and plaques and sculptures, Jacob is running and running.

Jacob came over to where I was sitting behind the desk and rested against me. I felt his warmth as I had on the day he was born and they laid him on my belly for me to feel him and for him, I suppose, to feel me. Now I felt his weight and his heart beating. He drew a long breath and laid his head upon my shoulder. I didn't want to put my arms around him to comfort him, because I thought that might indicate to him that I too perceived the moment to be heavy with a grief against which the two of us could only wrap our arms around one another, a grief so profound that only our bodies' warmth stood between us and desolation. I did feel as though we mourned the death of someone, as though we stood together before a monstrous stone, a tomb. I thought of Thetis, who said, as Achilles howled at the death of Patrocles, turning to the nymphs who filled the silvery cave at the bottom of the sea,

"Hear, sister Nereids, so you may know well
what pain is in my heart.

I am Misfortune, oh I have borne the noblest to
    misfortune,
for I bore a son strong and perfect, among
    heroes a hero,
and he grew tall as a tree, I raised him like a
    prize blossom
and I sent him away on the curved ships into
    Ilion
to fight the Trojans. And never again shall I
    receive him
when he shall have made his way homeward to
    his father's house.
As long as he lives and sees the light of the sun,
    so long shall he
suffer, nor can I do anything to help him,
even though I go to him."

And at the same time I wanted to laugh, because he
looked so tragic, and there is something grotesque about
the sight of a child oppressed with an old man's vision. I
wanted to laugh because I was upset. I felt tragic and oppressed, myself, but I didn't want him to know it. I didn't
want him to know that I can't see what replaces childhood
either. I didn't laugh, though. I didn't say anything yet;
my mind was racing, calculating, but he felt something,
because he said, "It's sad for you too. You don't have a
baby any more." But that was not what affected me. Nor
was I affected by the thought that he will indeed one day
go away to Troy and never come back to his father's house.
That is true, of course, but that is another story. The splin-
ter that had dislodged itself from the ordinary and was
working its way into my heart was the thought that he
wasn't a blessed creature, that his magic had deserted him,
that he had turned this way and that to find it again, but
it had eluded him. And in coming to tell me about it he
was acknowledging to himself that it was indeed gone and
not to be found again.

What had I thought? That he would dart here and there forever, escaping thus the net which had now fallen upon him, as it must on the best as well as on the others? Was it because he had played so brilliantly and for longer than the allotted playtime that I had indulged in thoughts of a kind of immortality for him? Mothers do just that over their sons, you will say. Yes, they do, you are right. Parents dream of tasting a kind of liberty in the joys they lust after for their children. I want to admit there is something embarrassing, even shameful, here. Here are things about which we cannot speak. We all move together in one inexorable swerve toward the end of our lives. We bear to one another different relations. To one, I am mother; to another, child or wife or friend. Some are of my age, we are agemates, and so look the same distance back and see the distance ahead shortening by the same degree; we are bound to one another by virtue of the fact that we stand on parallel rungs of our particular ladders; we understand that what is true for one of us is likely to be true for another, whether or not we dare to touch upon these facts aloud. Then there are those younger than ourselves, our friends whose youth we may envy, pity, despise, depending upon what we think they know about these matters. And then there are our children, whose upward curve warms and chills us, whom we would like to exhort to pleasure and to whom we would call out at the same time, *Memento mori*. No, not that. Surely not that. We would never have them think on death, nor would we have them see how we are ourselves aging, how we are the moribund at the wedding feast. But still we would warn them unbeknownst, so that in the midst of their shouts and games, with cheeks feverish with joy and lips parted to sing, suck, lick, or bite at the apple of life, they should still remember, and prepare, and bear forever the name of their lord and master, death, before their eyes, upon their sleeve.

"It's sad for you too, because you don't have a baby any more," he said again, to bring me back to him.

He sat down in the chair across from me.

"I wish I didn't have to grow up," he said.

There was a silence. I didn't know what would happen next. Then I told him that for adults there were pleasures to replace the ones children had. What were they? I said there was tennis. And skiing. Sports. Concerts. And travel. Cathedrals. Museums. And love, and having children of one's own. And I said that for some people work, and the effort and concentration of work, was a source of happiness. I said quite a few other things. I can't remember exactly what else I said. He did not ask me whether or not my work provided me with what we were talking about. But by now, for one reason or another, he was no longer pursuing the subject. His eyes were no longer tearful, but neither were they searching my own for some answer to these questions. He fiddled a little bit with the things on my desk, and I told him not to, and then he went off.

But when he was gone, I wanted to call him back. But to say what? He would probably have come back in looking stern, and asked, "What? What do you want?" And what was it I would say I wanted? I didn't want to have to detain someone eager to be off to the next thing while I tried to put into words for him something I couldn't even put into words for myself. I didn't want to submit to his gaze. I turned on my typewriter and felt it hum under my fingers, and I adjusted the margin release and thought with relief that I would at least get on with what I had been doing, but the moment faded and the humming turned into a buzz and I had to turn it off.

Outside it was neither afternoon nor night. A heavy uniform dull-blue light hung in the sky. The buildings were this color, although a little duller than the sky. So also, but darker still, were the pavement and the sidewalks. Except in the far distance where a remnant of afternoon gleamed a certain yellow green, the whole world was uniform, dull,

blue. I thought I would go out. I thought I could go out
to buy a bottle of wine for dinner. Or something sweet,
something chocolate, perhaps, for dessert.

In the bakery everything was brilliant and moist. Glass
shelves bore glowing little tarts. Lovely glistening hemi-
spheres of apricot rose out of pale custards. The warm air
was thick with vanilla and the choking fragrance of butter.
Women in furs and brown gloves reached for their white
boxes of desserts. I waited and saw myself reflected in the
mirrors and then reached over the counter for my own
white box, tied with a thin red string in a loop for my
finger.

But then I couldn't go straight home. Awkward as it
was to walk with the bottle of wine in its paper bag under
my arm and the pastry dangling from one finger, still
I walked and kept on walking. I was cold and getting
colder. At the park entrance I stopped and waited, but then
I went in.

By now all the blue had drained from the sky. In certain
spots old snow lay on the ground. I looked to see any
reddening of the bare branches, any swelling at the tips of
the twigs, any signs of spring at all. The reservoir was
framed with ice. I stood beside the frozen water holding
the bottle of wine against my chest.

On the blackening water I saw a dead swan lying, quite
near to me. A ruff of ice framed his body. His little head,
turned to one side, rested on the surface, and the big flat
gray bulge of his body was mottled and dirty and nasty.
One recoiled from the thought that he was cold and the
water was even colder, freezing cold. The entire world was
colorless, black water, gray snow, gray sky, gray swan,
and still, perfectly still. It was all texture, nuances of opac-
ity, of clarity, of light and of darkness, a black-and-white
photograph. I didn't at first notice that the water was moving. Slowly moving, pulled and pulling with it ice chunks,
humps of snowy ice, cracked shards of ice, plates of ice
broken off, old leaves flat and dirty, black shiny bits of

branch, and the big dead lump of swan, all moving, each following a path slightly different from the others, each one according to its own weight, size, buoyancy, so that one log turned a bit as it moved, another revolved, but all crept toward the neck of the pond where under a tangle of fallen leaves the water leaked into a lower wooded place. My fingers were aching. I was aware that I was on guard lest anyone appear and see me. It was as though I felt that I was doing something wrong, watching the dead swan, and I wanted to be alert so that if anyone came along I would have time to shake off my absorption, my own sense of moving downstream in a long cold dream.

I hadn't at first seen that slow turning of the water, or noticed that the skin of the pond was dragging with it like a slowly sliding tablecloth all the objects it carried: ice chunks, twigs, feathers, all sliding darkly away. But something about the swan, something about my thoughts about the dead swan, my sense of how cold he must be, of the chill of the water and the soddenness of his body, held me there in the dark afternoon, holding my awkward bundles with stiff fingers. Everything had seemed immobile, frozen, utterly still, and when I noticed the slight swerve of the floating world I felt my chilled body sway in response. I saw, as time slowed, that what had seemed frozen and fixed was in motion, that the poor cold swan and his dirty feathers and the little black twigs and the two black maple leaves, although they circled one around another, were nonetheless all moving in the same direction. The swan's body drew me to follow, and I walked as close to the water as I dared, leaving the path, and edging bit by bit to the far side. As the swan's body reached the far side of the pond it began to be carried a little bit faster and to turn in a slow spin, in tandem with a birch branch so soaked that its skin seemed not white but pinkish like gauze colored with blood and water. Together these two entered a spin that caused them to circle and bump each other, the swan seemingly heavier and passive, and the birch the aggressor.

Strange, that although they were nothing but stuff, one should scourge and the other suffer. Still, they reached an equality at last when with a sudden shudder each swung heavily as though to the pulse of a hidden conductor toward the dark place where the waters converged into a braid of water and together the swan and the birch tumbled away. Dead stuff.

Bloody crimson stung the sky in the dark air, and in the trees black twigs tapped and crackled and reached for one another over my head. I made a strange sound in my throat. I felt it come out of me and I heard it leave my mouth and wing away.

Intimacy

꙾ ꙾ Plump, sweet Lilly, with a baby in her belly and a baby on her lap, helplessly, vaguely undermines her man. Her dear baffled husband, at once brave as a bad boy and tearful as a kid, all warm arms and popping angers, quivers from time to time with the desire to punch his little wife, who gazes at him thereupon with wide dark tearless eyes.

At other moments he, if one could inquire and indeed if such questions could be answered, would describe with an eager enthusiasm a certain position of his wife's upraised arm that conveys for him all the secret vulnerability of her beloved body; a position that we might all observe on the beach in midsummer, seeing her strain to throw him a ball, back arched, elbow pointed to the sky, exposing to a burning sun the pale skin of her underarm, soft, untanned, naked. This same attitude is enjoyed by Stephen alone in moments of tender relaxation, when Lilly on her back lies resting, head upon her open hand, glance upon his face, her expression so slightly anxious and vague. Lying beside her then, Stephen, with one long relaxed leg weighing across hers, props his head on his raised hand. "Listen, Lil," he says. "Lil? Listen." With one finger he traces the main route of a long blue vein that tracks across her fat little stomach and disappears somewhere beneath her breast. "You liked it, didn't you? Lilly?" And Lilly may then kiss him very tenderly and draw the covers up around him.

In her turn, Lilly, if gently asked for the image that starts up before her eyes at the sound of "Stephen," would be flustered and yet proud to speak of her man, her dear husband. "Well, with his papers and law journals all around," she would say, glancing down, with a little secret smile. "At night. The lamp on, on the table, and him, you know, in the light. He sticks his feet all the way out under the table and scowls and frowns. You know, because he's thinking so hard." She will stop there, shyly in part and partly because she can't quite explain to us how it is that she comes into the room, sees him from the doorway, stands behind him, wants to bring him something—"Tea, dear?"—wants to touch his hair, kiss his bent neck; perhaps he would like to have the little bit that's left from dessert, so carefully folded in shining foil, just waiting to be wanted. She feels very deeply that it would be wrong of her to disturb him, although he might not be angry, might not even mind. But still.... The day is all done up, the baby is asleep and Lilly sits in the armchair and leans to pick up the paper, which she reads carefully page by page, with many little sighs and glances at Stephen's back.

It is almost night. Coffee cups and cigarettes drowned in sloppy saucers array the kitchen table. Four brown chrysanthemums nod over the rim of a glass. Clean cups hang from red hooks. On a high shelf, mournfully intense blue plates, so very beautiful, so very old, darkly reflect the pale autumn sky. Lilly is waiting for Stephen to sip his last cold sip. The child upon her lap, Margaret, dark-eyed like her mother and beautiful as her father, leans forward, playing a small game with burned-out matches, pushing them here, pushing them there. She sings a little song. Stephen looks up and smiles at her.

"May I take your cup, dear?" says Lilly.

Stephen reaches for one of the matchsticks and holds it before the baby's nose. Margaret looks at him out of the corners of her eyes. He wiggles the stick.

"Don't dear. I want to put her to bed. Don't start playing

with her now." He looks, frowning, at Lilly for a moment, and she raises her eyebrows.

Soon it will be cold in the kitchen. Soon the garden will disappear and the window will show only black. Soon, in fact, they will be depressed, night-sad. Stephen puts down his cup and rubs his head with both hands. Except for the child it is so silent. One hears the cup against the gritty saucer, the cooling oven creak and shrink. Far away, through trees and thin woods, a rare car whines on the highway. It is so dark.

Stretching creakily, Lilly gropes with her hand along the wall behind her head, feeling for the light switch. It is too uncomfortable, the darkness, the quiet. Stephen, hating intensely the sadness of the cooling world, catches his wife's hand. "Come. Come sit on my lap. Put her down. Come. Just for a minute."

"Oh, Stephen, really. Later." She mistakes his feeling entirely. Entirely? No, not entirely. Let us say, in part. Lilly stands up. Her apron bulges. "May I take your cup, dear?" she says. The little one sits on her hip, arms and legs clinging, eyes wide and exhausted. Legs in khaki pants crossed, big-shoed, chair pushed away from the table into the middle of the room, Stephen, with head bent way down, works his fingertips around and around in those hollows at the sides of his forehead, so often kissed and caressed at more tender moments by the attendant Lilly.

"Shall I take your cup, dear? Have you finished?" She holds the clinging child in both round arms, rubs her lips against that warm drooping neck, kisses that most delicate beloved softness. Slightly pouting her beautiful lips, Margaret, through half-closed eyes, watches her father. "Dear?" comes Lilly's soft question muffled in her child's black wispy curls.

Stephen stands, pushes over his chair, stamps to the table, picks up his cup and saucer, and brings them both down clanging on the porcelain sink. "Here. I'm finished. As you see."

Spills of coffee slide down the white sink walls. The silence that follows is of such profundity that one can hear the *pip-pip* of coffee drips hit the linoleum floor. Stephen and Lilly, however, cannot hear that delicate patter; each one hears only with the inner ear the mounting thunder of that outraged army of mercenaries and greedy tramps which, clamorous, invades the tottering soul, territory by territory, until it bursts into that final kingdom, the heart, and topples there its sovereign to rule in chaos and the misery of victory. All pacts, treaties, agreements, covenants, both domestic and foreign, forged in dogged labor of compromise and painful compensation, are, in this moment of despair, violated. Both Lilly and Stephen are trembling. That outward silence, which with the force of a glacier has caused them unknowing to step back from each other so that Stephen now presses himself against the sink and Lilly stands in the doorway with the staring child still wrapped around her, shudders and breaks.

Lilly gasps. As tears refresh her burning eyes, she turns and hugging closer the bobbing Margaret disappears swiftly in the dark of the hall. Her running footsteps shake the staircase. Doors open and close. Her voice is heard upstairs. Fat witch, thinks Stephen. Water drums in the tub.

With trembling fingers Stephen lights a cigarette. He drops the match on the floor. He sits down in Lilly's wooden chair and gazes at his own fallen one. Reaching out his leg, he hooks his foot about the rung of his chair and carefully, very carefully, without using his hands at all, rights it. He is waiting for his wife to come down to him. He holds the cigarette close to his ear and listens to it burn.

When Lilly returns to the kitchen, Margaret having been lingeringly soaped, rinsed, patted, bedded, kissed, and told with a quaver that Mama loves her and Papa too, very much, oh, very, very much, Stephen in a gesture of penitence and nobility has done up all the dishes except the pans, which he has piled out of his way on the floor. Rings of suds like ruffs circle his forearms. His face is red and he tries from time to time to wipe his wet forehead with his dry upper arm. The kitchen is steamy and damp from the hot running water. Moisture slides on the window-panes; the little kitchen curtains above the sink are limp.

Stephen didn't hear Lilly coming down the stairs because he was singing "Now Let Every Tongue Adore Thee" loudly and happily, soothed by the warm water and the clean dishes and the hustle and virtue of his activity. Grease and rage equally dissolved; order everywhere restored, where gleaming plates lean against one another and iri-descent bubbles sit in unrinsed glasses. He felt her presence, though, and turned quickly, afraid to see what signs of sorrow and reproach awaited him upon her face.

Lilly stands in the doorway. Who can count, who can in fact name, the little creasings, crossings, wrinklings, frowns, and blinkings that line and realign themselves upon her smooth face? What is she thinking? Is she angry still? Stephen peers into her eyes, his eyebrows raised, forehead as wrinkled as hers, suds dripping noisily from his wet hands.

She thinks he looks very dear and foolish indeed. "She's asleep, just about," says Lilly, temporizing still.

"I did the dishes," says Stephen, who cannot wait. "I though you would like it if I did." He wipes his hands on his trousers.

She is still waiting. He reaches for her hand.

"Lilly, please don't be angry with me."

"What do you mean? Of course I'm not angry. I just thought you... I just had to put the baby to... I mean I..."

Tears, again tears in those same old eyes wet and deep, quivering lips, trembling chin. She, guiltless, must now be forgiven. He, friendless, will be befriended. Stephen makes a little noise, half a sigh, half a moan, and each, with eyes shut, moves blindly toward the other. There, in each other's arms, enwrapped as though with blankets, quilts, and soft comforters, burrowing for solace, for depth of sympathy never to be unearthed, a demand is felt: a clamor, a desire known. They cannot see each other, their eyes are closed, but their hands like small animals in winter hunt feverishly for shelter: hers find his armpits, his the cave between her neck and hair.

They are standing in the middle of the kitchen swaying and sniffling. Water still rushes from the faucet and gurgles in the drain. Tears roll down the steamy panes. The kitchen clock buzzes.

Stephen's cheek rests on his wife's hair. An exquisite relaxation seeps into his body as her warmth meets him. He strokes her back; his hand circles around and around against her soft sweater. Half hypnotized he is; he holds her tighter and mumbles into her hair, "There, monkey, now don't cry. Don't cry any more." His hands, palms open, brush warmly her cheeks, throat, arms.

Damp, drained, happy, Lilly has stopped crying. She is drowsy with relief.

Still holding her with one arm, Stephen turns off the water, the light.

"Come on," he says and propels the passive, tear-doped Lilly down the dark hall and into the pillowed living room. There they sit on the couch, Lilly leaning against Stephen like a child asleep. They take turns sighing.

"Lilly, I don't know what happens," breathes Stephen, shaking his head. "It's so awful. It makes me feel so damn lonesome."

"There," says Lilly softly. "It doesn't matter. It's all over."

"There we were and you were so mad at me and I looked right at you and it was just like I didn't even know you." Stephen sighs again. "Do you know what I mean, to look right at a person and not even know them?"

Lilly looks right at Stephen but she doesn't know quite what to say. Look right at him and not even know him? Stephen? How could that be possible? Her Stephen? No, no; she knows only too well she is trying to fool herself. She knows what he means, but the truth is she doesn't relish the turn he is leading them on. Something is happening. Somehow the curtain of faintly narcotized comfort is lifting; Stephen is feeling better. He is refreshed, and Lilly shifts uncomfortably at the threat of the chill gust of scrutiny.

"What I mean is that I looked right at you and I just hated you," says Stephen, playing with her hair. He smiles at her dreamily. His face seems enormous. He lifts a handful of her damply curling hair and kisses her on the neck insistently. "So lonesome," he murmurs. "So awful." He sighs deeply. His hands reach around her waist and he rests his head upon her breasts. "Lilly, you do love me, don't you?"

"Of course I do. You know I do." But Lilly has seized upon his words. "Stephen, you're too heavy." She tries to move from under his weight. He said he hated me, she thinks, he said he hated me; and like a traveler who fixes upon a tiny spot on the far horizon, a buoy, another ship, to avoid the dizzying fact of plunging decks and lopsided seas, she focuses upon his words.

"Oh, I'm sorry. I'm always leaning on you. Come over here. This way, in my arms." And he smiles invitingly with a meaning look.

But Lilly, holding fast, shakes her head. "I'm not a thing," she says.

Stephen looks at her, troubled.

"Let's just sit here," says Lilly. She touches him on the cheek, afraid she has gone too far.

"All right," says Stephen.

Quietly on their fat couch they sit together for a moment. Then Stephen pulls the lamp's metal chain. He reaches for his book.

The bedroom is quite dark. Darkness clings like cloth to the walls, the ceiling, in the corners. The furniture looms.

A glimmer of the lesser darkness outside enters the window, slips dimly shining about the rim of the old pitcher, darkly brushes the mirror, polishes an edge of the curved bedstead, gleams about the pile of Lilly's dropped underwear, Stephen's shirt. In the bed they lie curled in opposite directions. Lilly's belly falls to one side; she cannot draw up her legs as she would like.

"Stephen?" says Lilly very softly.

"What?"

"Do you think the window is open too much? It's so awfully cold. And in the morning..."

"Do you want me to close it? I will if you want."

"Yes. Would you?"

Stephen sits up abruptly, sheets and covers flung this way and that, and feels his way to the window, which he partially closes with infinite deliberation.

"How is that?"

"Good. Stephen, come back in quickly."

He finds his way back into bed and Lilly reaches for his hand to squeeze. "Thank you, Stephen. Good night."

"Good night, baby," he says. He crumples one fat pillow beneath his head, another he holds tightly to his chest, his chin stuck well into its depths. Chill air settles on his cheek, his neck. He digs in closer to the center of the sheets. They are lying back to back. Their eyes are open. Lilly stares unseeing toward the garden full of sticks and branches. She thinks about their fight. They didn't really get over it. Maybe they really should have made love. Maybe that would have fixed it. She knows she mustn't say anything more about it, not even one more little hint or squeeze or anything. Oh, well, she thinks, but how sad she feels not to have things right.

Stephen watches little purple globes jump from the floor and slip upward, floating toward the ceiling.

All four feet are warming, and a gentle heat seeps into all folds of sheet and crumpled nightclothes. Thoughts and pulses slacken. Comfort is close by. Now follows a long stillness that no clock could correctly tick or stopwatch monitor, broken as Stephen and Lilly, waiting, awake, curled like watchful snails, at one moment burrow down deeper into their joint bed, move their feet, and feel, each one, the heat of the other. Their bottoms touch gently, pause and press closer, heart-shaped, unworried, warm.

They lie quite still. Lilly closes her wide eyes. Stephen sighs and closes his.

In her doll-strewn room the child turns over and sighs too.

The cooling house creaks.

All are asleep. Dreams begin.

Going to See the Leaves

ᔕ ᔕ

It was Mrs. Child's idea, to go to Vermont to see the leaves and to invite their son and his wife to go with them. They could stay, she said, in a really nice inn, and go for walks, and on Saturday, if it was warm, they could find a meadow to picnic in with a view of the mountains.

She had suggested the plan rather tentatively; there would be a lot of driving, and it would be sure to be quite expensive, putting up all four. Besides, she was hesitant about making outright proposals. She preferred to agree to the suggestions made by others.

"And on Sunday," she said, "there is a concert we might want to go to. And start home from there."

But Thomas agreed at once. He said, "Yes, let's."

Elizabeth felt that he had agreed too quickly; there was no chance now for her to explain why it was a good idea, no chance for them to talk about Luke and his wife, Sarah. Thomas said, "Yes, let's," in a voice that sounded as though he was putting his newspaper up before his face. Yes, they should go. Elizabeth needed something.

Elizabeth did want something. It had been at one time Thomas who used to say, "Let's take Lukie out West." He had suggested a trip to Kenya, to the Serengeti. One of his partners had gone there and advised him to go soon while the animals were still thriving and before Luke was too old to want to travel with his parents. Thomas's partner had said it would be the experience of a lifetime. But Elizabeth hadn't wanted to go and so they had stayed home and gone to the seaside for a week when Luke came home from camp. But recently Elizabeth thought about places to go—where, she didn't quite know—while Thomas now wanted to stay at home in the evening and on long weekends, as well as on his month's vacation.

Thomas did not know what made him agree so quickly to Elizabeth's suggestion. Still, the proposal struck him as one that would accomplish something that should be accomplished, touched his underlying understanding of things, for even to himself his "Yes, let's" sounded too quickly after his wife's, "Dear?"

Thomas drove, although Luke had offered to drive. After New Haven, they started north. A blue light, soft and even, spread from one part of the sky to the other. It was hot.

Thomas drove, looking straight ahead. Sarah sat behind Elizabeth, looking out the window. Her hair blew across her mouth. She pushed it away with the back of her hand. Luke turned this way and that, trying to find space for his long legs. His mother saw his profile and the full sculptured curve of his lips. He ran his big fingers through his blond hair, which sprang up again after his fingers had passed.

Elizabeth said, "We used to sing on drives."

Luke began: *"Oh, the cow kicked Nelly in the belly in the barn."*

Sarah: *"But the doctor said t'wouldn't do her any harm."*

The two young people sang out with their loud strong voices. They heard themselves. Their voices shook their chests and vibrated in their throats. Sarah tried to outsing Luke, she sent her voice from her diaphragm, a soldier in her cause. Luke heard the challenge but would have none of it. He had no doubt he could wrestle her to the ground, pin her, outsing her, but she would not accept this. Thomas sang with them, then fell silent. Elizabeth hummed.

They passed a clump of low red bushes on the grassy divider. Elizabeth said she hoped they had not come too early, that the leaves would have reached the height of their color.

They drove past the domes and cylinders of Hartford. There were many cars on the highway with out-of-state plates.

"I wonder how many of these cars are going to see the leaves," said Elizabeth. She had a strong response to the idea of people being brought together; the periodicity of things moved her, and the discovery of community in unexpected places.

Sarah opened her camera case. She loaded three cameras. "There," she said.

"Black-and-white?" said Elizabeth, looking over her shoulder. "For the leaves? Why black-and-white?"

"She takes a dim view of color," said Luke.

"Oh, Luke," said Sarah. "I want to try to do something with the leaves. With the light. I don't want just to gawk at the color."

"You know, in Japan, people swarm to the hillsides to see the leaves," said Elizabeth, while to herself she said that Sarah was not being rude to her, only eager about her work.

"Well, so do we. That's just what we're doing, isn't it? How is it different?" Luke pressed Sarah and his mother both.

"Nobody calls them 'leafies' in Japan," said Sarah.

"How do you know?" asked Luke. "How do you know there aren't just as many scoffers in Japan as here?"

"Peering out from behind screens and saying 'See the reafies' to one another." Sarah took up Luke's scenario with a certain excitement. She tried to adorn it, expand it, but Luke let it go, turned to the window, and Sarah's voice trailed off.

Thomas said nothing. He was the driver. He was the person behind the wheel, taking his wife where she wanted to go, ferrying the young people. It brought a sort of peace to him. He had, when he was young, harbored the idea of some outcome for himself. It had been unclear to him what it would be, but that it would be had seemed unquestionable. For most of his life, he had taken courage from the thought that a task awaited him. Thomas was still strong, still smooth-muscled and fit. Recently, the thought had come to him that perhaps the rest of his life would be no different from the way things were now, that he would not be called upon. Recently, he had found he could no longer contemplate his wife in an erotic fashion. Nothing was said about this. He meant to speak about it, but it seemed unspeakable. He could not raise the subject. He was not sure whether the reason was that he feared to hurt her or that he hesitated to embarrass himself. Sometimes he wished for old age when the issue would be, he thought, dead.

Soon they would pass Deerfield, where Thomas had spent his years from thirteen to seventeen. As the little school buildings came into view, Elizabeth, as she always did, turned her head to look at them across the fields. They seemed far away and very small. There Thomas had played ice hockey and read *Ethan Frome*. In the early morning, in all seasons, thick white fog had sat in the low places in the valley. In spring, limp yellow strings had blossomed on the birch trees. When his parents came to visit, they took him out to lunch in Greenfield. His father asked him how things were going. His mother told him what his cousins and aunts were doing. He felt very small, very young. It seemed at each visit that he and his parents were growing farther apart. He no longer cried when they left. He knew it was untenable to love them.

"How come you didn't send Luke to Deerfield?" asked Sarah.

"Thomas hated Deerfield. They snapped towels at him." Elizabeth was always outraged that his parents had sent him off so young and tender.

But I didn't hate it, Thomas was thinking. That he had been lonely as a child had seemed only ordinary. He had merely waited for the end of childhood.

In school, he had walked from building to building. He had seen, as the morning fog lifted, the color of the leaves, which had grown stronger during the night. No child remarked to another on the color or observed aloud that the trees, which had been green when school started, were now orange or red. The children noticed the leaves but said nothing.

In the autumn, he had run cross-country; in winter, he wrestled. He grew, he felt himself to be merely the container of his strength. Who could tell how much stronger he might become? Running through tunnels of copper leaves, he thought of nothing but persisting. In winter afternoons in the wrestling room, he heard the thunder of the basketball team overhead. In January, the daylight was gone by the time he got to the gym. Under yellow lightbulbs in their metal cages, he lifted weights and practiced his moves. On Saturday, all honed and pure, he struggled with another youth. His veins swelled. He scarcely saw his opponent. It was all in terms of something else. If I win this match, then... what? His thoughts carried him far, but something lay beyond them. There was something more than the trophy to be gained.

In the rearview mirror Thomas caught his son's glance. Father and son seldom spoke to one another, but each sometimes intercepted the other's gaze. Now Thomas swung out into the passing lane and pressed the accelerator to the floor, causing Elizabeth to sway forward against her seat belt and the maps to slide along the top of the dashboard. Exhaust fumes entered the car as he passed first one trailer truck, then another, and pulled back into his lane.

"Thomas, my goodness," said Elizabeth.

As they crossed into Vermont, the color in the trees intensified.

"Oh, look," said Elizabeth, as they left the Connecticut Valley and started up into the orange hills, "this really is the peak. We came at the right time."

In the morning, Thomas and Luke got up first. They met in the hall, testing the locks of the doors they were closing upon their wives, who had not yet risen. Sunlight blazed at a little window at the end of the hall. Thomas waited for Luke to reach him. He felt a shy excitement which he was scornful of, but nonetheless he wondered what he could offer Luke that might please him. Luke approached, bending a little under the low ceiling of the hallway, and together they went down the uneven, carpeted stairs to the dining room.

In the morning light, between butterings and bites and swallows, Thomas examined his son. He felt able to look at Luke in a way he could not in his wife's presence. He was anxious to make his observations acutely and quickly, before Elizabeth should appear. Luke's skin was fresh, he looked rested, but what Thomas had thought he had detected yesterday was true: his hair was beginning to recede. Thomas reached up to his own hairline, but he blurred the gesture by stroking his head where the hair was still thick.

How old is Luke? he thought. Is he twenty-five or already twenty-six? Thomas hoped he was only twenty-five.

Luke held his fork with the tines down and pressed a neatly cut, five-layered mound of pancake into the maple syrup that had pooled at the outer edge of his plate. When the syrup had all disappeared into the pancake, he leaned over his plate and brought the forkful to his mouth. It was winking with syrup. When he had finished, he drank the last of his milk, tilting the glass, and then turned to his coffee.

"Good?" said Thomas. "Did you enjoy your breakfast?"

"Listen, Daddy," said Luke. "I know you are worried about me. And Mommy is too. I know that. But don't. Or do. I know you can't help it. I will be all right."

The morning sun moved in the sky just enough to brilliantly strike the water glasses and the restaurant silver on the table, flinging blades of light on the walls. The tablecloth was too white to look at. For that moment Thomas felt that Luke was the father and he was the son. He wanted to say something to Luke that would be true. At the same time he wanted to say something that would make him be the father again. He raised his eyes from the quivering light and saw that Elizabeth and Sarah were standing in the doorway of the dining room.

"There you are!" said Elizabeth.

Thomas and Luke stood up. Elizabeth wore a white cardigan over a blouse with little lavender dots, and a blue denim skirt. She was wearing pink lipstick. Her "There you are!" had sounded so loud in the dining room that she was surprised. She crossed quickly from the dim hall to the bright square of sunlight where Thomas and Luke were standing, letting herself smile only when she had reached them. Sarah followed. She wore an olive shirt with many pockets. When she moved her head, her long straight hair parted in places, and Luke could see the little turquoise earrings his parents had given her. She seldom wore jewelry, and he was glad she had put them on.

"How lucky we are!" said Elizabeth and smoothed her skirt under her as she bent to sit down on the chair Thomas was holding. "What a beautiful day it is!"

Luke winced at the eagerness and timidity with which his mother, dressed like a child, had crossed the room. Both his mother and father had blue eyes. To Luke, it seemed that they both peered at him as if to see what was inside his head. Their look seemed to try to exact something from him, some agreement; for instance, as now, that it was indeed a beautiful day, and since all were agreed on that, all of one mind, some further harmony was bound to follow. The mild questioning look of his mother and father peering at him made him say, "Let's get this show on the road," but when he realized that his mother and Sarah had not even ordered yet, he sat back, abashed.

Thomas ordered Granola for Sarah and muffins for Elizabeth. While they ate, the men drank more coffee, and together they agreed on a plan for the day.

After lunch, it took a while to get comfortable. They shook the crumbs off the two blankets and spread them out again to rest on, but they had picnicked in a mown field and the ground was stubbly. Finally, they moved the blankets to the far edge of the field, under the trees where the grass was soft. Thomas was reluctant to leave the car so far out of sight, but Luke said he wanted to take a nap and Sarah had her tripod and filters ready and was eager to get to work. For a while, as they carried the blankets across the field, sending up showers of crickets with each step, it seemed they were making too much fuss. Elizabeth tried not to seem to be arranging things. She knew there could be a reaction against her for being too managing, too motherly, but she was willing, right now, to risk it. What had they driven all this way for, if not for this? Nonetheless, as they walked, she hung back, not to be first. Thomas took the lead, and Luke walked with him. The sun shone through the rims of their ears. Sarah noticed this and said to Elizabeth, "The sun is shining through their ears." Elizabeth was offended that this young woman should speak so familiarly about her son's ears, her husband's.

"I think Luke might go back to school next semester," said Sarah in a soft voice. Elizabeth knew she was anxious lest Luke hear them talking about him.

When the blankets were smoothed out, Luke stretched himself out on the plaid one and folded his arms over his chest.

"Night," he said from under closed eyes.

Sarah looked at him, the length of him on the blanket, occupying it fully.

"I'm going to take some wide-angle shots," she said, with a lift of her chin, and she picked up her tripod and bag and stalked off down the field.

And so, when Elizabeth and Thomas lay down on their blanket, having carefully made room for one another, the family was together, mother, father, and son.

After a bit, Luke opened his eyes and turned his head toward his mother. She was lying on her back with her eyes closed. The afternoon sun struck her full in the face. A lavender vein moved stepwise across her eyelid. The lid was rose-colored; the edge of the lid looked moist and it trembled slightly. Her yellow-gray hair lay in flattened coils under the weight of her head. Above her upper lip fine hairs shone in the light, and from the red cave of her nostril long yellow hairs emerged. Luke touched his own nostril and felt the stiff hairs that stuck out of his nose. He raised himself on one elbow and looked beyond his mother. His father lay beside her. Briefly, he saw them both up close, enormous, as though in a fever, or through a lens. Their faces were magnified in his eyes; for a second they occupied the entire landscape.

With a guilty heart, he sat up straight and felt in his buttoned-down shirt pocket for a marijuana cigarette. At the sound of the match striking, both his parents opened their eyes. As he inhaled the smoke, his father said, "Do you have to do that, Lukie?" and he said, "Yes, Daddy, I do."

He sat with his knees up, one arm around them, holding his cigarette with his free hand. His parents sat up and began to brush bits of grass off their sweaters. Leaves the color of apricots, with an occasional speck of light green, were falling from the tree above.

"There's Sarah," said Elizabeth.

Sarah was at the lower end of the meadow. It was difficult to tell how far away she was. She looked tiny, and there was nothing to measure her by.

Elizabeth stood up and waved, but the sun was behind her. "Saaa-rah." She gave a sort of yodel. Sarah turned in their direction but Luke knew that all she could see was the afternoon sun. They watched her walking up the slope with her awkward, determined stride. She could as well have been an utter stranger.

Luke gently tapped his cigarette on a rock in the wall

behind him. When he was quite sure it was out, he pinched the end and folded the remains in a bit of paper, which he carefully returned to his shirt pocket. Then he stood up and in long strides ran the length of the field to Sarah, who was standing at the edge of the woods in a drift of leaves. She watched him running toward her. The opening and closing of his legs gave her the impression he was running in slow motion and she started to reach for her camera, but he got to her too soon, before she was ready. She hadn't got the lens cap off when he grabbed her and held his arms around her. "Oh, Sarah, don't leave me," he said. She felt his heart leaping like an animal in a cage; she smelled his sweat and felt the moisture on his neck and face.

"I wasn't going to leave you," she said, but she felt, as usual, a certain confusion, an apprehension. Why had he lain down in the field in front of his mother and father and taken up the whole blanket? Didn't that mean she should leave him? How could they be going to lead their whole lives together? Where was comfort to come from, where was happiness? From passion? Perhaps, but it was unreliable. Who was this man, this blond man? How had she come to lie down with a stranger?

The sun was veiled, as a thin skin of clouds rose in the west. As the light in the sky paled, the radiance of the leaves increased. Something solemn and important was happening in the woods. A chill crept over the meadow. Luke's lips nuzzled Sarah's neck. His knee pressed between her legs. She saw the small figures of Elizabeth and Thomas leave the far edge of the field and move toward them over the stubble. Luke inserted his hand under the waist of her jeans in the back and reached down to feel her buttocks, thin and clenched.

"Luke," said Sarah, twisting about, "don't. Don't do that."

Luke began to laugh. He wanted to wrestle with her, to push her down in the leaves. The smell of the woods rode upon the cooling air that poured into the meadow, carrying with it the smell of moss, of mushrooms, of rot, of black mud, of rotting stumps and the rotting bodies of small animals, of chipmunks, rats, mice, squirrels, of everything that dies in the woods. The smell of decaying leaves and decomposition was delicious; it appeared suddenly and turned thoughts to the secrets that lie in the forest. Luke pressed against Sarah.

"Later," said Sarah.

"I would like to go into the woods with you now," said Luke.

He pressed his knee against the hard double seam of her blue jeans. She stepped back and let herself fall to the ground. The wind blew a hard gust. Above, the ash tree let loose a shower of leaves, yellow, the color of dark mustard. They lay in the leaves, laughing.

"OK," said Sarah, in a soft voice, as Luke's parents, smiling uneasily, drew near, "later."

The wind blew all night long. Elizabeth slept and woke, hearing the wind and the tap of branches against the window of the unfamiliar room. She lay in bed and thought about the leaves and their drying stems and the trees they dance upon as they try to leave. She thought about how hard it is for them to leave. The tree sends juices, the leaf clings; the wind blows and the leaf turns, spins, bends back upon its stem.

She went to the window and stood looking out. Her bare feet on the wooden floor made her feel like a girl. The room was cold. She heard the wind and saw that the leaves were still falling in the dark. It was a grave matter that all the leaves were falling, but she was very glad she had come to see them.

The concert was played in what had been a Congregationalist church, square and white, which had been renovated to accommodate its new function. Molded stackable seats replaced the pews, and recording equipment stuck out of the pulpit. On the floor, wires trailed.

It took most of the first movement for Elizabeth to begin to concentrate. She had to remind herself to pay attention to the sound that drummed or gurgled in her head, memorably, she thought, but no sooner had the first bit opened into its development than it was gone. And she couldn't get it back. She criticized herself, but at the same time wondered if she was alone in this failing or whether there were others like herself who were confused.

The cellist plucked a loose strand from his bow and poised himself to plunge in again. The cello was pale, almost yellow; the viola was red. The two violins were similar in color, but one glittered, the smaller one. The second violinist was a woman who wore a long dress of bright green. The dress was sleeveless and the woman's arms were white. Elizabeth thought it was no doubt a convenience for her not to have sleeves. A loose sleeve would get in the way, and a tight-fitting sleeve would pull under the arms or at the elbow. And yet the young woman was exposed, and her arms seemed very private, with everyone looking on. Of the four players she was the only woman. She was neither pretty nor ugly. From time to time, as she played, she gave her head a shake, and her smooth brown hair crested and fell back into place. The first violinist played, and she waited, holding her violin upright on her thigh. When he had played for several measures, she raised her violin and held it under her chin, letting the bow hang loose from her right hand, watching the other players and nodding her head, until, with a sudden deliberate movement, she lifted the bow and began to play vigorously. Her thin arm went rapidly up and down. The four leaned toward one another as they played. The music was loud and strong. Then the three others plucked their instruments and the woman in green played alone.

Afternoon light fell in stripes upon the listeners. In the darkness between the stripes, motes of dust floated. Elizabeth held her breath. The music rose from the platform and spread to fill the space above. The sound resonated upon whatever it touched: the beams in the ceiling, the planked floor, the walls. The first violinist and the woman in green were playing sweetly and loudly to one another, while the others sustained them with arpeggios. As he finished drawing his bow and with a subtle gesture of his wrist was preparing to return it, she was drawing hers to its tip. Her head was bent down so her chin touched her chest, and her arms were spread wide apart. Her face was hidden. Only the top of her bowed head could be seen. The sounds she was pulling from her instrument were the sounds of tearing, the sound of something long being torn in two. The cello and viola fell silent and then the first violinist stopped playing as though to honor the last of her long trembling notes. Elizabeth thought, Then there is no happiness. A rush of courage filled her completely, and she thought, I can bear it, now that I know.

From above a peculiar noise distressed her. She realized it had been pressing upon her for some time and she had been resisting it, as though holding a door shut against a great force, but now she gave way. She looked up. On a ledge under one of the high windows, birds were sitting. One fluttered out, circled, and landed. The others chirped and shrilled. It was a shocking breach. Could the players hear? Elizabeth would have liked to do something to save the situation, but that was ludicrous. What could she do? Nothing, she thought, but sit there and wait it out. Distracted, she waited for the quartet to finish.

When the concert was over and the players had come back several times to bow to the audience, which was standing to applaud, Elizabeth turned around to look up at the eaves. The birds had disappeared, but she thought she saw straw sticking out from one of the high joists. The glare of the lights caught a feather that was floating down in an uneven way, impelled by whatever drafts reigned up there.

Luke followed her glance. He put his arm around her. "Did they bother you, the birds?" he said.

Love for him weakened her. She wanted to sit down. She did not want Thomas to see how moved she was, or Luke either.

"Sparrows, were they?" she asked, turning her face away slightly to hide her eyes.

"*Passer domesticus,*" he said, evoking thus the days when he and she had walked together, noting the particulars of the world. She had carried with her her bird book and little jars in which to bring home beetles or whatever special things they should find. In this manner she had felt she was molding him into the kind of man she dreamed for him to become.

In the parking lot, they saw the cellist set his instrument carefully in the back seat of his car. They said how glad they were that they had already checked out of the inn, so they could start for home at once. Thomas agreed that Luke should drive, and he and Elizabeth sat in the back.

Thomas reached for Elizabeth's hand.

"I am glad we came," he said.

"Oh, wonderful," said Sarah. "Thank you so much. Thank you both."

Thomas fell asleep holding Elizabeth's hand. When she saw that he was deeply asleep, she gently withdrew her hand. Darkness gathered quickly. As the light sank out of the air, the sky became dark blue. Sarah and Luke murmured together in the front seat, laughing occasionally. Then they fell silent. Sarah leaned her head on the headrest. Soon she too was asleep. Elizabeth looked at the red taillights extending far ahead and the sweep of the lights of the northbound cars approaching. By the dim light of the dashboard she could see the line of Luke's cheek and his brow when he turned his head to look in the side mirror.

"Mom?" said Luke softly. "Why don't you go to sleep too? I'm going to drive very carefully."

"I wasn't worrying," said Elizabeth, quite truthfully, but nonetheless she too then fell asleep.

Although they had agreed to stop for a bite to eat somewhere near the halfway point, Luke did not stop at all. He drove peacefully, absorbed in the task of not driving too fast or too slowly, in deciding whom to pass and whom to let pass, checking the fuel gauge and the mileage. No one woke until he stopped for the toll at the bridge. Both his parents woke then, and after a minute Sarah too raised her head.

"Where are we?" asked Elizabeth.

"Almost home," said Luke. "You were asleep almost the whole way."